CLOSE PROXIMITY

EVERNIGHT PUBLISHING ®

www.evernightpublishing.com

Copyright© 2019

Erin M. Leaf

Editor: Karyn White

Cover Art: Jay Aheer

ISBN: 978-0-3695-0016-8

CLOSE PROXIMITY

THE ELEVATOR

Close Proximity, 1

Erin M. Leaf

Copyright © 2018

Chapter One

"Come on, come on," Adrian said, pressing the key for the elevator. While he waited, he loosened his tie and sighed, relieved that the workday had finally fucking ended. He'd had to stay late. Again. And he'd had to handhold the team, talking them through the revision control process again. They'd managed to screw it all up anyway, hence his late night, fixing all of their mistakes. And where was his boss? Out playing golf on Long Island somewhere. Again.

He looked at his phone, then growled when the damned battery beeped and it died right there in his hands. He glanced back up the hall to the double doors that led to the open concept office of his company. He kept a charger at his desk, but he'd forgotten to plug his phone in, and he really didn't want to go back and wait around for it to come back to life.

"Screw it," he muttered, shoving it into his pants

pocket. He didn't need to know the exact time. He knew it was after eight on a Friday night. Sure, he could hit a bar, or call up a friend or two and hang out, but honestly? All he wanted right now was his bed. *And maybe a quick hand job so I can sleep well instead of tossing and turning,* he thought, grimacing. *At least I have the weekend off, for once.*

He stared at the brass doors, but they didn't open. *Do not press the button,* he told himself as his hand twitched. It wouldn't help. It never helped. It was simply human nature to keep pressing the button over and over again, but he'd be damned if he'd be one of those people. When the down arrow finally binged, he rolled his shoulders and waited. When the doors slid apart, he hurried inside before they fully opened and stabbed his finger at the lobby button. "Time to go," he muttered, already thinking about how good it would feel to take off his shoes and sprawl on the sofa with his air conditioner turned on full blast. Manhattan's latest heatwave was making everyone irritable.

"Late night?"

The hair on the back of Adrian's neck prickled. *Was that—* He spun around. Oh, yeah, it *was* Mr. Hottie Lee from the top floor. Adrian willed his dick to stay the hell down, but it was a close thing as he took in the twinkle in the older man's warm brown eyes. They'd said "hello" on the elevator often, and he'd seen the man here and there in the building, but they'd never managed a conversation. From the rumors Adrian had heard, Mr. Greyson Lee was a nice guy, but stern if you crossed him. Given that he dressed like a billionaire, Adrian could understand how Mr. Lee's demeanor might intimidate some people, but he'd always found the guy absurdly hot.

And he's waiting for you to respond, so stop

daydreaming about taking off all of his clothes and focus, he told himself as he cleared his throat. "Hey, Mr. Lee. I didn't see you," he said, wincing when his voice cracked.

Mr. Lee smiled. "I can be stealthy when I have to."

Stealthy? Adrian had no idea what the man was talking about. Mr. Greyson Lee was the man who'd occupied most of Adrian's jack-off fantasies for the past year, ever since they'd first met in this very elevator. The man had to be at least forty, given the hint of silver in his dark hair and beard, but he certainly didn't look like he was fifteen years older than Adrian. Greyson Lee's height and bulk always surprised him. Weren't Asian dudes supposed to be short? But then, rumor had it that Greyson Lee was biracial, so perhaps that explained the man's height. *You need to stop listening to every rumor you hear,* he reminded himself. *And stereotyping people isn't cool, either.* He felt his face heat up. He hated feeling this awkward.

Mr. Lee leaned back against the railing and crossed his arms, showing off his bulging biceps. He had his dark button-down shirt open at the throat and rolled to his elbows. "You should tell your bosses not to work you so hard."

With difficulty, Adrian tore his gaze away from the hint of a tattoo he saw on Mr. Lee's forearm. "Ha, yeah. As if. I'm the only one who seems to understand revision control," he said, rolling his shoulders again, more from frustration than anything else. He'd been riding this very elevator with this guy at least once a week for the past year, and they never got beyond small talk. *Even if he's queer, he's way out of your league, Adrian.* He swallowed, feeling like a fourteen year old. He reminded himself that he was a twenty-five-year-old professional software engineer, but it didn't help.

"Ah. That's tricky stuff, Mr. Hughes," Mr. Lee said, half smiling. He looked like he had a secret.

Adrian grimaced. "Please. It's not that difficult. All they need to do is follow the process I wrote out. In great detail." He shut up and forcibly pushed away thoughts of work. If he didn't, he'd be up all night worrying about what the others on his team would break next. "What about you, Mr. Lee?" he asked instead, wondering yet again if the guy was straight or gay or what. Mr. Lee had great hair, and amazing taste in shoes, but that didn't mean diddly. He should know. Adrian was as gay as you could get, and if his sister hadn't helped him pick out his clothes, he'd probably go to work wearing jeans and a black t-shirt. He had *zero* fashion sense. "It's Friday, and it's late, and yet here you are." He smiled. "Stuck on an elevator." From the corner of his eye, he watched the numbers on the display count down. Thirty-one, thirty, twenty-nine…

"Mr. Lee? That sounds like you're talking to my father," The older man chuckled. "We've been riding the same elevator for months. You can call me Greyson."

Adrian forcibly battled back a blush, mentally cursing his fair skin. "Then you need to call me Adrian," he managed, wondering if he looked as ridiculous as he felt. He gripped his laptop bag tighter. *Like a security blanket,* he thought, annoyed with himself. He really sucked at the whole social interaction thing.

"Adrian," Greyson said, voice dipping into a lower register.

Adrian lost his war with his dick. Thank God his bag covered his erection. "So," he began, searching for something witty to say. Anything, really, would do, but his brain stuttered to a halt when he caught Greyson staring at his hands. *What the hell is he looking at?* he wondered, and then the elevator lurched to a halt so abruptly that he nearly dropped his laptop as his arms flailed out. He stumbled, and then Greyson put his hands on him, steadying him as the elevator shuddered.

Adrian sucked in a shocked breath, not sure if he was freaking out because the damned elevator *broke* or because Greyson was practically on top of him. The older man smelled like coffee and cologne, two of Adrian's favorite scents. His dick swelled even more, and he tightened his fingers around his bag until the handle creaked. A sharp clang sounded from somewhere above them, and then the lights flickered off. "Oh, shit," he said, as the emergency lights clicked on. "That's not good."

Greyson grimaced. "Are you okay?" He didn't let go of Adrian's arms. His hands were very warm.

Adrian looked at him, mind racing down a dozen inappropriate alleyways. "What just happened?" he finally asked, reminding himself not to lean into the guy. *He doesn't want you climbing him like a tree, idiot.*

Greyson let go of Adrian and ran a hand through his hair, mussing up his neat style. Adrian wanted to brush back the longish strand that fell across Greyson's forehead so badly that he took a step back before his hands reached out independently of his brain.

"My guess? Brownout," Greyson said, sounding resigned. "This heatwave is messing with the power grid." He made a face. "Life in the city," he added wryly.

Adrian's biceps felt oddly light after Greyson's strong grip. "That's bad. That's very, very bad." He wasn't claustrophobic, but he didn't relish being trapped in a small box with no way out, and no way to know when they'd be rescued. "My cell phone died right before I left work."

Greyson pulled his out of his pocket, then frowned as he looked at the display. "Huh."

"What?" Adrian waited for Greyson to call for help. "What does 'huh' mean?"

Greyson held his cell phone out, showing Adrian the blank display before sliding it back into his pocket. "My battery is at zero."

Adrian blinked. "Wait, what? How is that possible?" What were the odds of *both* of them having dead phones at the same time?

Greyson sighed. "It's possible because I forgot to plug it in this morning, and I had meetings all day." He shrugged. "I often forget to charge it. I don't usually have time to fiddle with my phone during the day."

That makes sense, dammit, Adrian thought, disgusted with himself all over again for forgetting to plug his in. "Today is the first time I've ever forgotten to charge mine," he heard himself say, as if from far away. Meanwhile, his brain was racing in circles, yelling, *I'm stuck in an elevator with Mr. Hottie!* over and over.

Greyson raised his brows but didn't speak. Instead, he walked over to the panel and popped open the emergency phone slot. "Hello? Hello? Anyone there?" He waited a beat, and then put it back on its hook. "It's dead." He pushed the emergency button a few times. Nothing happened, and he snorted. "Not surprising. I've been nagging building maintenance for the past three months about the elevators, but it takes forever to schedule service."

"No." Adrian absolutely could not accept that he wasn't going to get to go home and pass out on his damned sofa after working all damned day on stupid shit at his job. "No, I refuse."

That startled a laugh out of Greyson. "You refuse?"

Adrian flushed, and this time he didn't bother trying to battle it down. "This is crazy." He shifted his laptop bag from one hand to the other. In the dim light, he couldn't see Greyson's eyes clearly, but he imagined the amusement in them. "What are the odds we'd be stuck here like this?"

"The odds are high, I'd say." Greyson unbuttoned two more buttons on his shirt. Smooth skin and the hint of another tattoo peeked out from behind his lapels.

Adrian stared at the view and then sighed. "Damn." He put down his bag and took off his suit jacket. The elevator was cool for now, but it wouldn't stay that way. "How long do you think we'll have to wait?"

Greyson shrugged. "It's after eight PM. I doubt anyone will come looking for us for a while." He rubbed the back of his neck tiredly. "I know that there are a few people still working on the tenth floor."

"On a Friday night?" Adrian couldn't imagine what they'd be doing.

"Call center," Greyson said.

Adrian nodded. That made sense. "Well, then, I guess someone will figure out that the elevators are stuck when one of them decides to get food." He sighed. "Eventually." He eyed Greyson, then flushed all over again. The man looked seriously hot, even at the end of a long day, at the tail end of a long week. "So."

Greyson leaned back against the railing again. "So?"

Adrian wracked his brain for something intelligent to say. "How about those Mets?"

Greyson burst out laughing. "Oh no, we are *not* going to talk about sports. I might be a workaholic, but I'm not so cliché that the only topic of conversation I can do is baseball."

"Well, thank God for that. I don't know a damn thing about sports." Adrian grinned. "How about the weather?"

Greyson rolled his eyes. On a man his age, it looked ridiculously attractive. "Seriously? You're going with the weather?"

Adrian swallowed down his lust and continued. "Politics? Climate change?"

"I think climate changes falls under the weather cliché," Greyson countered, half smiling.

Adrian sighed theatrically. "Then I've got nothing." He undid his tie completely and pulled it off, and then stuffed it in his bag, not caring that the tail of it hung out. The air was growing warmer, and if he didn't take precautions now, he'd be a puddle of sweat within a half hour.

"Your tie has numbers on it," Greyson said, sounding surprised. "I thought that was a random print."

Of course he would notice that. Adrian made a face. "Yeah, yeah, I'm a geek." He pulled on the tail and held it up. "It's pi. See?"

"Pie? It doesn't look like dessert to me." Greyson's voice held amusement.

The man is playing with me, I know it. Adrian shook his head and explained anyway. "No, the number pi, not the food. I really should save it for pi day in March, but I can't resist. I love a good geeky tie, and I feel the need to share it with others as often as possible."

"You don't look like a geek," Greyson said.

"I'm a software engineer working late on a Friday night on revision control. If that's not the definition of geekiness, I don't know what is." Adrian stared at the older man. "What does a geek look like, anyway?"

"Thick glasses, scraggly beard, maybe a man bun if he's trying to be a hipster," Greyson said, and then he chuckled. "Pocket protector. You don't have any of those. I would've noticed."

"A pocket protector," Adrian echoed as he rubbed at the stubble he'd forgotten to shave this morning. He had light brown hair, so it wasn't terribly obvious when he skipped a day or two. "I don't even know where I'd get one of those." He found himself smiling, too, because it was clear that Greyson was teasing him. *Who'd have thought that the quiet, intimidating Mr. Greyson Lee would be so charming?* he thought, once again fighting with his libido. This guy grew more and more attractive with every word he uttered. "And a man bun. No. Just … no." He couldn't even imagine doing that with his hair. His sister would laugh and laugh and laugh. No thank you. He ran a hand through his locks self-consciously. His hair wasn't long, and it wasn't short. It was in-between, and rapidly approaching annoying. He'd have to get it cut soon.

"Well, you have the computer bag thing going for you, and a nerdy tie, so you're not a totally lost cause as a spokesman for the engineers of the world," Greyson said, looking him up and down. "Though, that suit fits you surprisingly well for a geek."

"My sister—" Adrian began to say, but then his stupid voice cracked again. Greyson's gaze was lingering on his groin, and Adrian hurriedly shoved his hands in his pockets and tried again. "My sister helps me pick out my stuff. I'm hopeless at fashion." He made an abortive move to wave at himself, and then realized he'd best leave his hands in his pockets. *Where they can hide this damned erection. At this rate, I'm going to pass out from blue balls long before I suffocate in here from lack of air.*

"Ah. I'm an only child, so I have to do my own shopping," Greyson said, glancing down at himself. "I fumble along okay."

Adrian took in the man's beautifully tailored grey slacks and dark purple shirt and sighed. *Fumble along?*

Is he for real? The grey highlighted the silver in Greyson's dark hair, and the purple brought out his warm skin tones. "You look fantastic." Adrian's gaze dropped to the older man's thighs, and it took a supreme act of will to not stare. Greyson's clothes hugged him in all the right places, and the man was built. "Seriously. Those colors look great on you." He clamped his mouth shut before he could keep babbling. Greyson smirked at him again, and Adrian went still. *Wait a second. Is he flirting with me? Straight guys don't talk about clothes in an elevator.* "So," he said again, inanely.

"So." Greyson smiled. "Are we giving up on the small talk?"

"Are you flirting with me?" Adrian blurted out, and then immediately wished he could stuff his entire fist in his mouth. *God, why am I so damned lame?* He nearly groaned with embarrassment.

Greyson's smile faded, and he took a step closer. "Took you long enough to figure it out."

Adrian blinked, still grappling with the shame of his social idiocy. When his mind caught up to the meaning of Greyson's words, he had to search for a response. "What?"

"Yes, Adrian. I'm flirting with you." Greyson put an arm against the wall over Adrian's head, and loomed. "Is that okay?"

Adrian looked up at him. *Shit. He's taller than me,* he thought as his mouth went dry. "Uh…" The ability to put words into sentences fled.

"You seem startled by this." Greyson reached out and touched a finger to the hair currently slipping into Adrian's eyes. "Did I read you wrong? Are you straight?"

Adrian swallowed, and shook his head. Then nodded. "No. I'm not straight." *I'm completely fucking out of my depth, is what I am,* he thought, imagining himself flailing in the deep end of a pool. He couldn't swim for shit, and this was exactly what it felt like when he'd had to take the can-you-float test in swimming class in high school.

"I'm bi," Greyson said, casually, as though he picked up nerdy guys in elevators all the time.

"Um," Adrian said, still trying to wrap his brain around this situation. Mr. Greyson Lee, his private crush for the past year, and possibly super-rich entrepreneur, was flirting with him. In an elevator. That they would probably be stuck inside for God knew how long. "I didn't know."

Greyson dropped his arm. "That's why I'm telling you." He straightened up. "Are you not interested? If not, I'll back off."

"No!" Adrian almost lunged for the guy. His hand landed on Greyson's shirt.

"No?" Greyson's eyes twinkled again. "You want me to stop?"

"No, I don't. I mean, yes. I'm interested," Adrian said, fast and breathless. "Damn. You really threw me for a loop, man." He scrubbed a hand over his face. "Is it hot in here? I think it's getting hot in here."

Greyson chuckled. "Yes, it's hot in here. The power in the building is out, and it's at least ninety-five degrees outside. But that's not why I'm hot." He reached out again and touched Adrian's lips. "You work too hard."

Holy shit. He's sexy. Jesus God help me. Adrian manfully resisted the urge to bite Greyson's fingertips. "Why do you say that?"

The finger fell away. "Because it's almost nine o'clock on a Friday night, and you're trapped in here with me." Greyson cocked his head. "And you look tired.

I've seen you leave work late more often than not."

He's been watching me? Adrian had no idea how to respond to that. "Can we just go back to the flirting thing?" He really didn't want to talk about work. He didn't want to even *think* about work.

"Sure." Greyson moved a little closer. "You have really blue eyes."

Adrian had no idea what to say to that. "Uh, thanks? So do you." He swallowed nervously. "I mean, you have really nice eyes, too. I know they're not blue, although it's hard to tell because the light in here is terrible right now. And you have amazing hair." *Oh my God, shut up, before he starts to think you're a total loser,* he told himself, teeth clenched shut.

"It's hair. I'm getting old." Greyson chuckled, then rubbed his chin. "You really don't know how handsome you are, do you?"

Adrian shook his head. "Are you for real? Since when do you pick up guys in the elevator?"

Greyson lost his smile. "Since never." He straightened up. "I don't usually do this, but you seem really chill. And I like you. You're always polite, every single time someone speaks to you. Not everyone is, in this city."

Adrian stared at Greyson, completely taken aback. "That's because no one can hear the swearing inside my head. I'm not really that nice."

Greyson smiled. "I think you're too modest. If you weren't nice, you'd say all the things you're thinking out loud."

Adrian had no response to that and decided to keep his mouth shut in order to prevent further inanities from escaping.

"To be perfectly honest, I haven't been on a date in years." Greyson grimaced, suddenly looking not nearly as confident. "I'm not great at the whole dating thing. And I'm usually very busy. It's not easy to meet people when you're stuck in meetings all day."

"Yeah." Adrian's nerves calmed down considerably. "Well, I'm not great at it either." He looked around the dim elevator and shook his head. "Serendipity?"

Greyson laughed. "So, you're saying that it took us being locked up together in a tiny box to get to this point?" He glanced at Adrian's bag, still clutched in his right hand. "That's pretty sad."

"Dude," Adrian said, feeling much better about, well, everything. He set his bag down. "We've been greeting each other in the elevator and halls for a *year*. But neither of us said more than 'hello'. If that's not lame, I don't know what is."

Greyson tugged on Adrian's left arm, until he let it slide out of his pocket. Adrian's erection hadn't flagged, not through the awkward conversation nor the mutual acknowledgment of flirting, but for some reason, he wasn't nearly as self-conscious about it as he had been earlier.

"I won't tell anyone if you won't," Greyson said. He used Adrian's arm to draw him in, like a man tugging down a kite stuck on a thermal: slow and steady and relentless.

Whoa. He might think he sucks at dating, but he's top-notch at seduction, Adrian thought as Greyson brought his arm up to his shoulder. "Who would I tell?" he managed to say as his fingers touched soft hair. He let them slide into the soft strands like he'd wanted to do for forever. The prickle of Greyson's beard tickled his wrist. He wondered what that would feel like on his cock, and nearly groaned aloud.

"What are we talking about?" Greyson asked

softly, leaning closer.

Adrian looked into the older man's eyes. The warm brown had gone dark with arousal. "I have no idea," Adrian said, right before Greyson's lips met his.

Chapter Two

Adrian lost the ability to breathe the moment Greyson's tongue slipped into his mouth. The hint of bourbon on the edge of the coffee he smelled earlier was without a doubt the sexiest taste he'd ever experienced in a kiss. He wrapped his left hand around Greyson's head, sinking into the soft strands of his hair, and wrapped the other one around the man's bicep. "Fuck," he moaned, when Greyson slid his mouth to the corner of his lips and sighed.

"Not in the elevator," Greyson said, and Adrian choked on a laugh.

"No, I'm not into public exhibition," he said, wondering wildly if there were security cameras in here. He glanced up at the ceiling but didn't see any tech that might indicate a hidden lens.

"No cameras are working right now," Greyson said, kissing him again.

Aw, fuck it, Adrian thought as Greyson's strong, warm body pressed him into the brass railing. It hurt a bit, but he didn't give two shits. "Jesus, Greyson." He bit the older man's plump lower lip, then sucked away the sting. "You're killing me."

"Ha," was all Greyson said, but then his hands were unbuttoning Adrian's shirt. "Nice," he said, when the lapels gaped open. He put a hand on Adrian's chest. "You work out."

Adrian couldn't remember if he worked out or not. He could barely remember his own damn name. "God, don't tease me." He wrapped a leg around Greyson's calf and brought their groins together. When their erections touched, he groaned. He needed to get off so badly his hips jerked without his conscious control.

"Fuck," Greyson muttered, hands dropping to

Adrian's ass. He ground them together, pushing Adrian into the railing even more. "I haven't been this worked up in years."

"This is crazy," Adrian agreed, hips rolling into Greyson's. He kissed the older man again, then shoved him away. "Stop."

Greyson froze. "Stop?"

Adrian already had his hands at the older man's pants. "Unbutton, you stupid fucking— Ah." He breathed easier when the inside button popped off and didn't feel even a hint of regret as it pinged off the wall and rolled into a corner. He was too busy unzipping the placket and reaching his hands into Greyson's boxers. "Jesus, you're big."

"Yeah, just like that," Greyson said, voice dropping even lower.

Adrian wrapped his fingers around Greyson's cock and stroked. "How are you so perfect?"

Greyson made a sound halfway between a laugh and a moan. "I'm not even close to perfect."

Adrian let go and unbuttoned the rest of Greyson's shirt, pausing to take in the amazing tattoo inked all over his chest. "Wow." He slid his palms all over the smooth skin. "That's fucking gorgeous. A dragon?"

Greyson shrugged. "My father was fond of dragons. Said they were good luck."

Adrian nodded. "I want to lick you all over."

Greyson laughed. "By all means." He leaned back, arms open. He should've looked ridiculous, standing there half dressed with his cock pointing out, but he didn't. He looked like a warrior emerging from modern clothes: fierce and hot and quietly menacing.

"Don't poke the dragon," Adrian murmured as he went to his knees. He pressed a fist to his erection, hoping like hell he wouldn't go off like some teenager out for his first ride.

"I'm no dragon," Greyson said.

"Yes, you are," Adrian replied, leaning in and inhaling the musky scent of him. *God, he smells good.* He rubbed his cheek against Greyson's cock, and then took it in his hand. "I'm going to suck you until you forget your name." Greyson exhaled, and Adrian licked his cockhead. "Fuck, you taste good," he said against the soft skin, and then he closed his eyes and opened his mouth. Hands sank into his hair as he slid down, scrubbing his tongue along the shaft. When it hit the back of his throat, he swallowed, then relaxed. He could do this. So what if he was seriously out of practice? He *wanted* to deep throat this man. He wanted Greyson to lose his mind, and he wanted to be the reason.

"Oh my God," Greyson croaked, sounding strangled.

Adrian swallowed again around the cock in his throat, then slid off, slowly. "I'm not a god," he said, smirking up at the older man.

Greyson blinked, then smiled. "No, but you have the mouth of an angel."

Adrian flushed, and covered his embarrassment by sucking Greyson in again. He rolled the older man's balls gently, then pressed up behind them. He'd only been going at it for maybe a minute when Greyson shuddered, then roughly dragged him off and pulled him to his feet.

"What—" Adrian stuttered.

Greyson swallowed his question with a kiss. "You're fucking playing with fire," he said, biting Adrian's lip, hard. "Damn." He kissed him again, ravaging his mouth. When he slipped his hand down and roughly undid his pants, Adrian's knees nearly buckled.

"This is insane," he said, hanging onto Greyson for dear life. How the man opened his pants with one hand he didn't know, but in the next second Greyson had his fingers around his cock. Adrian couldn't control the jerk of his hips. Greyson's hand wasn't as soft as he'd expected, and the little bit of roughness nearly sent him over the edge then and there.

"Fuck, yeah. That's it," Greyson murmured. "Come on, Adrian."

Adrian groaned, head dropping to Greyson's shoulder. He could barely make out the outline of his hand, but he didn't really need the visuals. He could feel every damned inch of Greyson's palm on his cock. "I'm so close."

"Good." Greyson jacked him fast and hard. "Come all over me."

Adrian moaned. "I wanted to suck you."

Greyson laughed. "I had maybe a half second to get you off me before I blew it. I want more than a minute-long fumble in the elevator from you."

Adrian's skin prickled. He understood the words Greyson was saying, but the meaning wouldn't sink in around his arousal. "Please, don't stop." He gripped Greyson's arm. It felt hard as iron and just as strong.

"I'm not stopping," Greyson said, shifting his weight. When he moved his hand away, Adrian protested, but then Greyson leaned back and gathered Adrian close, lining up their dicks. "Here, lean into me."

Adrian let Greyson's body show him where to go, and the next thing he knew, Greyson had his hands wrapped around both of them. His cock swelled, and he knew he was not going to last even another minute. "Shit."

Greyson smiled tightly, and he twisted his grip, and Adrian stopped trying to hold back. Nothing was going to stop this train. He grabbed onto Greyson and snapped his hips forward, once, twice, and then that was it. Pleasure rolled through him, hot and hard, and Greyson growled, kissing him through it. Dimly, Adrian felt Greyson shaking, and then the older man's cock jerked. Warm jizz coated them both as Adrian shuddered along with him. His cock pulsed again, and then again, wringing him completely dry in the midst of a small, stupidly hot box in the middle of midtown Manhattan. He slumped against Greyson, hoping like hell the older man could hold him up or they'd both end up on the floor.

What seemed a long time later, but was probably only five minutes or so, Greyson started chuckling. Adrian lifted his head, blinking at him. "What?"

"We just got off on an elevator." Greyson was smiling. He didn't look like a dragon anymore. He looked like a dragon who'd just eaten an entire box of donuts: satisfied and vaguely surprised. "This isn't my usual method of going on dates."

"You said you don't usually go on dates," Adrian pointed out.

Greyson shrugged, and Adrian slid off his shoulder. He caught himself on the wall, then made a supreme effort to stand up. He succeeded. Mostly. His legs still felt a bit wiggly. "Yeah, we got off. So what?" He felt a certain amount of smugness. He knew quite a few people, women *and* men, who would've loved to be in his shoes right now. Mr. Greyson Lee was an ongoing topic of speculation and wishful crushes because of his looks, his supposed money, and unfortunately, his racial background. Half the people Adrian knew wanted to sleep with him, and the other half felt that a guy with his ethnic background shouldn't be working in their building. No one knew what Greyson's company was, or exactly what it did, but it didn't seem to matter. Adrian was one of the few people who knew Greyson regularly rode the elevator to the top floor. *Whatever. I have what they want. Haters gonna hate.* He grinned at the older man. "I'm not sorry." He glanced up involuntarily. "Even if there are cameras in here."

"There aren't any cameras. I checked when I first bought—" Greyson suddenly stopped talking and looked sheepish.

Adrian raised an eyebrow. "Bought what?" He glanced down and grimaced, then tried to dab at the mess on his groin with his shirttail. It didn't help. He looked up to find Greyson half smiling and holding out an honest to goodness starched handkerchief. "Thanks," Adrian said, taking the cloth. It worked a lot better than his shirt. He wiped himself off, then rolled up the cloth. "Bought what?" he asked again. He had a feeling he knew the answer, but he wanted to hear the older man admit it. He held out the handkerchief.

"This building," Greyson said after a pause. He took the cloth and tucked it into his pocket. "I bought it six months ago. That's how I know there are no cameras in here, and that the elevators need to be upgraded." He glanced at the emergency phone dangling uselessly from its hook.

Adrian stared at him. "You bought the building? The entire building? A forty-story building in midtown Manhattan?" The cost of such a thing boggled the mind. "Jesus." How rich was this guy? He glanced down at himself again, then tucked his cock away. He felt strangely like he'd just had sex with the pope. If Greyson could afford to buy an *entire building*, the guy's semen was probably worth its weight in gold.

Greyson was smiling again. "Yes. The entire building. I like the location." He'd already buttoned himself up, too, sadly. Adrian would've liked to get a better look at the older man's spectacular tattoo, but the light in here was crap, and well, who knew if he'd get another chance to ravish the man? He felt vaguely guilty when he saw the missing button from Greyson's pants in the corner of the elevator. "Macy's is just up the block. And there's a good Korean restaurant around the corner," Greyson said, as if that made any sense.

Adrian shook his head. "You liked the location." He ran a hand over his face. "You're richer than God, then?"

Greyson laughed. "No, I'm not that wealthy. I'm simply lucky." His smile fell away. "My father left me quite a bit of money after he died." He grimaced. "Guilt money, I call it. I made a few good investments. That's all it is."

Adrian frowned. It didn't sound as though Greyson had enjoyed a good relationship with his father. Adrian thought of his dad, singing as he cooked the family dinner. His parents had been very cool with his sexuality. His little sister had never even known anything was different about it. He hadn't even had to really come out. Everyone had always known he was gay, not that he walked around broadcasting it. And he didn't talk about it at work, because his orientation was no one's business but his. *And not everyone has the kind of family you do,* he reminded himself. "I'm sorry," he said, feeling weird for apologizing. The man owned the damned building. *But money isn't everything.*

Greyson looked at him for a moment, then smiled softly. "Thank you. I had a feeling you'd understand. My father and I didn't always get along."

Adrian flushed. "Yeah, well." He looked around, and then as suddenly as the lights had gone out, they snapped back on. He lurched as the elevator shuddered and resumed its descent to the lobby. Cool air blew on his face as the fans kicked back on with the elevator. "Whoa."

"Just in time," Greyson said, smoothing a hand over his hair. "We might have confessed even more awkward things if we'd been stuck in there any longer."

Adrian smirked, but Greyson wasn't looking at him. A pang of uncertainty fluttered in his chest, but he pushed it down. *The guy doesn't owe me anything,* he reminded himself. "Yeah. Like, you might've found out that I'm too socially inept to go on actual dates. Or that I've never had an actual boyfriend."

Greyson lifted his eyebrows. "I don't have any trouble talking to you."

"I'm okay one-on-one, but when I get in a group of people I have a tendency to trip over my own words." Adrian grimaced. "It's embarrassing."

"Then how in the hell did you get so good at giving head?" Greyson asked.

Adrian flushed. "Uh." He had no desire to answer this particular question. An image of his favorite dildo flashed across his mind. "Natural talent?"

Greyson laughed, and then the doors opened, saving Adrian from further trauma.

"Greyson, thank God," a young Asian man exclaimed the moment the doors opened enough for them to exit. He looked almost like a younger version of Greyson. "I've been calling you for the past half hour!"

"My cell phone died, Andrew," Greyson said, glancing at Adrian. "And then the elevator froze when the power went out."

"Tell me something I don't know. I've been arguing with the power company for the past fifteen minutes," Andrew said, frowning down at his tablet. "But you're late for that dinner with the people from—"

"Yes, yes, I realize that," Greyson said, interrupting. He made a face. "I'll have to catch up with you later," he said to Adrian, then glanced at the young man who'd accosted them. "When my assistant isn't about to lose his mind."

Andrew snorted. "I've already lost my mind, working for you. If we weren't related, I would've quit years ago."

"No, you wouldn't have," Greyson said.

"I might've. If Mom hadn't flipped out at me," Andrew said.

Greyson rolled his eyes. "Aunt Margaret would never do anything so impolite as 'flipping out'." He used air quotes to emphasize his point.

Andrew nodded. "True, true."

Adrian didn't know what to do: *Ask him for his number? Duck back into the elevator?* He'd swear he could feel drying jizz on his hip. His face heated at the thought. *Talk about awkward.*

"Come on, Grey. I have the car waiting," Andrew tugged at Greyson's arm.

Greyson sighed. "Later, Adrian," he said, starting to follow his assistant. They both swiped out at the security gate. Halfway to the door, he pivoted, walking backwards. "You owe me a button." He pointed at Adrian, then turned and walked out of the building.

Adrian blinked as Greyson disappeared down the sidewalk. He didn't know the first thing about sewing a button back onto a pair of pants. Maybe his sister did? He glanced around the foyer. At the desk, the security guard gave him a shrug.

What just happened? Adrian rubbed his face as the usual post-orgasm afterglow faded, leaving him feeling weirdly anxious. He looked back into the elevator. The button he'd popped off Greyson's pants sat in the corner. He ducked inside and grabbed it. It didn't look like much. It was just your usual grey, dress slacks button, but for some reason, it felt heavy as a stone when he slipped it into his pocket.

Chapter Three

"Okay, what gives, Adrian? You've been moping around all morning," Jeannie said, sliding a perfectly rolled crepe in front of him. "I made these to cheer you up. Eat it and tell me if it's crap."

"You didn't make these to cheer me up. You made them because you're getting tested on Monday." Adrian's stomach rumbled, but he didn't feel like eating. They sat in the kitchen of their parents' apartment in Brooklyn. Adrian always stopped in on Saturdays, when his sister had no classes. Today his parents were off visiting relatives, so it was just him and Jeannie. He rolled the button he'd saved from the elevator encounter around his fingers, then forced himself to stop and yanked his hand out of his pocket. It was just a stupid button, right?

"Eat," she said, giving him the look of death that siblings were so good at.

"All right, all right. It looks delicious," he said, lifting his fork. He knew better than to refuse to try his sister's latest creation. She liked to test out her work on the family before she had to recreate the recipes in culinary school. He usually enjoyed being her guinea pig, but today he just wasn't in the mood. He cut into the crepe, then moaned when the sweet confection hit his taste buds. "Okay, wow."

"Wow good, or wow bad?" Jeannie asked.

"Are you kidding me? It's fucking delicious," he said, shoving another bite into his mouth. Maybe if he kept chewing he wouldn't have to answer her questions about why he was acting so moody.

"Good. Hopefully I'll get an A this time," Jeannie said, sliding out a chair and sitting down. She folded her hands and rested her elbows on the table. "Now, tell me what's got your panties in such a twist."

Adrian glowered at her. "I don't know what you're talking about. I only wear boxers." He shoved another large bite into his mouth.

"TMI! I did *not* need to know that." She glared at him. "You've been sighing the entire time I've been cooking, Adrian. It's annoying." She leaned back in her chair. "Spill. What's going on?"

Adrian shook his head, still chewing. He pointed to his mouth, miming an inability to speak.

"Oh, please. Like you've never talked with your mouth full," she said derisively. "Usually when you won't talk to me it's because you're embarrassed."

Adrian's face heated as he thought about Greyson, *again*. He hadn't been able to sleep last night until he'd jacked off to the memory of the older man's delicious cock in his mouth. "No," he said, cutting another piece of crepe. "I'm not talking about it."

"Oh, ho! Did you get laid, big brother?" Jeannie crowed. "Your face is positively glowing!"

Adrian felt his balls shrivel up at the thought of his sister knowing anything about his sex life. "None of your business!" He pointed the fork at her.

"It's my business if you're going to come over here and act like someone ran over your puppy." She grinned at him. "You know I'll just keep nagging you."

Adrian finished chewing the last bite of crepe, then pushed his plate away. "Fine. You asked for it." He rolled his shoulders, trying to get rid of the tension in his neck. "I met this guy in the elevator last night. We got stuck in there together when the power cut out." He shrugged. "We talked. The end." He looked away so his sister wouldn't see he was holding information back from her.

"You talked? Yeah, no. I don't believe you,"

Jeannie said, pursing her lips. "You wouldn't be this squirmy if all you'd done was talk." She leaned forward. "Did you hook up? Did you get his number?"

Adrian groaned. "Jeannie, please. Just drop it, okay?"

She shook her head. "Uh-uh. Why are you being so weird about it? You're twenty-five. It's about time you met someone."

"He's forty, okay? And rich. And hot. And I didn't get his number," Adrian finally said. He could tell by her expression that she was not going to let it go. "He said he'd be in touch, but both of our cell phones were dead, so we couldn't exchange numbers. Ugh." He pushed his hands through his hair. "And then his assistant dragged him off to some dinner meeting. It was awkward. And weird." He made a face. "Did I mention awkward?" He sighed. "I don't know if I even *want* to pursue anything with him. We don't exactly run in the same circles."

"Wait, you hooked up with a rich, older man? Whoa." Jeannie's eyes sparkled. "I did *not* see that coming."

"Yeah, well, it doesn't matter. I'll probably never see him again," Adrian muttered. That was how his hookups usually went. He'd never yet met a guy who was interested in more than a hand job. As soon as they found out he was a nerdy engineer, most guys went running the opposite direction.

"Why would you say that? You have a lot to offer a guy. You're smart, you have a good job—" Jeannie began, but stopped when Adrian laughed.

"Jeannie, the guy owns the building I work in." He didn't know how to put it more bluntly than that. Greyson Lee was *way* the hell out of his league. "It's not like he cares if I have a good job or not."

"Wait." His sister blinked at him. "I know you said he was rich, but I thought you meant he was some sort of normal rich person, not a zillionaire."

"Yeah, well." Adrian grimaced. "He's a zillionaire. And hot as hell. It's a disturbing combo."

After a long pause, his sister shook her head. "Well, at least you can say you once hooked up in an elevator on those silly online tests. That's got to count for something." She stood up and started gathering the dirty plates. "I mean, I got thirty points on one those quizzes because I hooked up on an airplane, once."

"Jesus, Jeannie! No. Just stop right now," Adrian said, clapping his hands over his ears. "I do *not* want to hear about your hookups. And also, what are you doing having hookups? You're too young to date."

"Bro, I'm twenty-two, not twelve." His sister laughed as she put the dishes in the sink, then came over and gave him a hug. "Have a little faith, Adrian. You have no idea what might happen."

Adrian returned the hug. "You're annoyingly optimistic, sis."

Jeannie grinned. "Because I know what a great guy you are. Maybe Mr. Rich Dude will surprise you."

"Uh-huh," Adrian said, not wanting to contradict her, but he couldn't muster up the same hope she had for his dating future. He had too long of a history of weirdness and lack of dates to really believe that Greyson Lee would look him up.

****

Monday morning saw Adrian standing outside his work building, glaring at the glass doors. The bustle of Manhattan, which he usually found soothing, grated on him today. The bodega on the corner didn't have the cherries he was hoping to buy for lunch. And most of all, he didn't want to go inside and risk running into

Greyson. He'd spent the rest of the weekend freaking out over their elevator encounter, in between cleaning up yet more messes from the software team. He hadn't relished spending all of Sunday online, rewriting code remotely, but he hadn't had much choice. Their project's deadline loomed closer and closer.

"You're a geek loser with no love life," he muttered to himself. Greyson hadn't tried to call him. Adrian had tried looking up Greyson's number, but people that rich didn't make it easy for random plebes to get in touch. He'd gone to sleep convinced that Mr. Hottie Lee wanted nothing to do with him, and now Adrian had to go to work and risk running into the man in the halls. *Because my life isn't already incredibly awkward, right?* He shook his head and forced himself to push open the doors.

"Adrian! Hey, I was waiting for you," Bethany said the moment he walked inside.

Adrian stopped short, then grimaced when two people following him into the building nearly ran him over. "Sorry," he said, getting dirty looks in return. He sighed and moved further inside the marble interior. He'd always liked the marble, but today it just seemed crass. "Hey, Bethany."

He wished he'd called in sick. He could've faked something—sore throat, vomiting, near death experience—right? Bethany had been pursuing him for months and didn't believe him when he told her he wasn't interested. He really ought to report her for harassment, but didn't feel like going through the hell that would entail with HR.

"I was hoping you were free for dinner tonight," Bethany said, completely undeterred by his scowl. Her perky grin irritated the shit out of him.

"I can't. I'm busy," he said shortly, striding to the

elevators after he swiped in and walked through the security gate. He nodded to the guard, who gave him a sympathetic grin, then joined the crowd in front of the brass doors. He had a feeling that she was one of those women simply looking for a nice guy with a stable job, and who could blame her? He wanted the same thing. She wasn't the worst girl he'd ever met, but she was damned persistent.

"Maybe tomorrow, then?" Bethany pushed the button for him.

I can't get away from her, either, Adrian thought irritably. She worked for his company, in the marketing department. "Bethany, I'm sorry, but I'm not interested." He gave her a weak smile as he reached out and banged on the up button. The frustration of work, plus Bethany, plus no call from Greyson had pushed him right to the edge. He knew pushing on the damn thing wouldn't call the elevator any faster.

"It could be a working dinner, if you can't get free early," Bethany said.

Adrian stared at her. "I don't understand why you're so persistent," he finally said. "You realize you're harassing me. If you continue, I'll have to involve HR, and I don't think either of us want it to get to that point."

"Girls can't harass guys," she said as she stepped closer and put a finger on his chest. "And I'm asking because you're cute."

Cute? Is she serious? Ugh. Adrian leaned back as she leaned in. "Bethany—"

"Good morning, Adrian."

Adrian froze as the sound of Greyson's voice made every last hair on his body stand up and take notice. "Greyson, hey," he said, trying to play it cool. He couldn't tell if he felt flustered or aroused. *Maybe both?* he thought, eyeing the two people he least wanted to run into at the same freaking time. Would Greyson be able to tell he didn't like Bethany? Would he care?

Adrian didn't know what to do. A wave of anxiety swept through him as he struggled with the kind of awkward social situation nightmares were made of. *Worst. Monday. Ever.*

"I'm sorry I didn't get in touch with you this weekend. I was called away to Seattle on business," Greyson said, smiling at Adrian.

Adrian stared at Greyson's impeccable grey suit and pale blue shirt. He'd accented the outfit with a royal blue tie. Did the man ever look anything less than delicious? "Um, okay." He pushed the button again, wishing the floor would swallow him up. He really, *really* wanted to give Greyson a chance to explain, but he felt beyond weird talking to the guy with Bethany breathing down his neck. He could feel her glare burning a hole through his head.

Greyson's smile slipped as he clearly picked up on the tension. "Is everything okay?"

"Adrian, honey. Who is this?" Bethany asked, leaning into him.

Adrian ground his teeth as he tried to extricate his arm from her grasp. He shook her off. "I'm having a bit of a difficult Monday, Greyson." He stepped back, less concerned than he should be that his move unbalanced Bethany. She shouldn't have been hanging on him in the first place.

"Adrian, what gives?" Bethany's voice slid up two octaves. "Who is this?"

Greyson looked at her, eyes narrowing. He moved forward, standing closer to Adrian than was strictly polite. "Do you work with Adrian? He's never mentioned you to me," he said to Bethany. His tone implied the kind of familiarity only a boyfriend would have.

Bethany flushed and opened her mouth.

Before she could reply, the elevator opened. Adrian grabbed Greyson's hand and dragged him onto the elevator, pushing ahead of the waiting crowd. Luckily, he caught Bethany by surprise, and too many other people stepped on before she could, and then the doors closed.

"Whew, close one," Adrian muttered. When he looked up, Greyson was looking at him with a hint of amusement on his face.

"That girl looked at you like you were a winning lottery ticket."

Adrian laughed unwillingly. "That's … actually not far off the mark. She keeps asking me out. She doesn't seem to understand that I'm not interested."

Greyson smiled. "And soon to be taken, I hope."

Wait, what? Adrian frowned. "You didn't call. I tried to look you up, but your number is impossible to locate." He shook his head. "I thought—" He stopped short and swallowed the frustrated words that wanted to come out. "I don't know what I thought," he muttered finally, glancing around. Most people on the elevator pretended not to hear conversations, but that didn't mean everyone couldn't hear every word. The last thing he wanted was to provide a show.

Greyson's smile faded. "I know, and I'm sorry about that. I really did want to call you, but the Seattle trip was completely unexpected." He lifted a shoulder. "And my number is unlisted." He tilted his head and smiled again. "Can you do dinner tonight? My treat. I'll make it up to you."

Two dinner invites on one day? This never happens. Adrian's stomach flipped. The man smelled fabulous, and after Bethany's cloying perfume and the funk of midtown in the middle of summer, Greyson's scent intoxicated him. "I don't know," he said, still thinking about his shitty weekend. "We're from two different worlds, Greyson." He glanced around, hoping no one was listening in, but no such luck. He could tell by the expressions on the people around him that *everyone* wanted to know about his love life. He grimaced. Fortunately, the elevator stopped, and half the people got out. Adrian was about to leave, too—*so what if I have to walk up ten flights of stairs to get to work*—but Greyson touched his arm.

"Please, let me try again," he said, softly. "I really would like to get to know you better. I feel terrible that I wasn't able to see you this weekend."

Adrian hesitated as the memory of Greyson's cock in his hands flashed across his mind, and then the door shut. He blushed, consigning the hottest memory of his life to the back corner of his brain. *Now is not the time, Adrian.* He needed to think about what the guy said, and not just because Greyson was gorgeous. *He really does seem apologetic.*

The older man held his gaze, then reached out and tapped the button for the top floor. Three of the other five people dropped their fake disinterest and stared at Greyson via the polished brass reflection of the doors. Adrian glared back until they looked away. No one used that button, and everyone knew it. That button was reserved for the building's owner, AKA Greyson, not that anyone ever saw him use it. Adrian wasn't even sure that the others knew that Greyson was the owner. He hadn't known, after all. He frowned. "Wait, what are you doing here during rush hour? I only ever see you in the elevator at lunchtime."

"I'm getting in late because my plane just got in this morning," Greyson said. "And you dragged me in here, remember?"

Adrian crossed his arms over his chest, jostling the strap of his laptop bag. "I didn't drag you into the elevator on Friday night." He stared at Greyson.

Greyson rubbed his chin. "No, you didn't."

Adrian looked away. Greyson clearly wasn't going to explain himself. "I need to get to work." The elevator stopped. The rest of the people got out, but Greyson snagged Adrian's shirt sleeve.

"Adrian, wait."

Adrian sighed. How hard-to-get did he really want to play this? *Not very,* he admitted privately. Greyson hadn't even done anything wrong. *I don't want to play hard-to-get at all. So what if my feelings were hurt when he didn't call? I'm a grownup. And Greyson is a good guy.* He let the older man pull him back further into the elevator. "I'm sorry," he said, watching the doors close once again. "I'm in a crappy mood. Bethany has been getting on my last nerve, lately." He smiled wryly. "And it's Monday."

Greyson chuckled. "Monday, Monday."

Adrian nodded, trying to push off his crankiness. He had a hot, rich older man begging him for his time. What the hell did he think he was doing, being all disgruntled? "So," he said, leaning back against the elevator's railing. "I told my sister about you."

Greyson lifted an eyebrow. "And what did she say?"

Adrian shrugged. "She said that maybe you'd surprise me." He grinned, then. "And that at least I could say I once hooked up in an elevator."

Greyson laughed, then very deliberately took a step back, reached out, and pushed the emergency stop button.

Adrian grabbed the railing as the elevator lurched

to a stop. "What are you doing?" He glanced at the number stuck on the display: thirty-nine. One floor below the top. Was Greyson crazy? It was the morning rush hour and he'd just taken one of the busiest elevators offline.

Greyson stalked over to him. "Now you can say you hooked up in an elevator twice." He took Adrian's laptop bag by the strap and set it on the floor. Before Adrian could protest, Greyson leaned in and kissed him. Adrian groaned, opening his mouth. Greyson's tongue slipped inside. He tasted like coffee, and cinnamon.

Adrian tore his mouth away, gasping. "Were you eating cake for breakfast?"

Greyson grinned. "A cinnamon latte." He leaned in again, nibbling down Adrian's jaw. "And now I'm going to follow that up with you."

"What? That makes no sense." Adrian reached out for the railing. His legs were none too steady. "People are going to be freaking out over the missing elevator."

"There are five others they can use." Greyson dropped to his knees and undid Adrian's pants.

"Oh my God." Adrian stuffed his fist in his mouth and bit down as Greyson eased out his erection.

"I haven't even done anything yet," Greyson said, and then he sucked Adrian's cock into his mouth.

Adrian moaned. The older man's mouth was hot and wet and perfect. He stared down, and when Greyson tipped his head back to look at him, Adrian almost lost it then and there. "Oh fuck," he stuttered, shivering. "Greyson—"

Greyson slid off but slipped a hand into Adrian's pants to cup his balls. "Let me blow you. This is my apology for not calling you this weekend." Greyson bent back down, and this time he deep throated Adrian's erection, as if it were easy.

Adrian gripped the railing so tightly the bones of his fingers hurt. His hips jerked as Greyson sucked. When, the older man reached back and pressed the spot just behind his balls, Adrian stifled a groan.

"Just let it happen, Adrian. I can't keep the elevator stopped all day," Greyson said. He licked the head of Adrian's cock. His mouth was red and wet, and he looked like something out of a porn video. "How fast can you come?"

Adrian exhaled. "With you? Really fucking fast."

Greyson grinned, and sucked him back in.

Oh, my fucking God, Adrian thought as an orgasm suddenly came out of nowhere. He couldn't stop it. He couldn't do anything except stand there, completely fucking undone by Greyson's perfect, hot, wet mouth. He made a sound in the back of his throat, trying to warn the older man, but Greyson didn't let up. He swallowed around Adrian's cockhead, and it felt so damned exquisite that Adrian saw stars. His knees buckled, and Greyson caught him around his thighs, pinning him to the wall. Adrian's cock swelled even more, and somehow Greyson sucked him through it, swallowing and sucking until Adrian shuddered. He put his hands on Greyson's hair and tugged when it became too much. The older man smiled and eased off, waiting as Adrian shivered through the aftershocks, and then he tucked him back into his pants. While Adrian stood there, completely shell-shocked, Greyson zipped Adrian up, then stood and kissed him lightly. "Mmm. Nice."

Adrian stared at him. "You—"

Greyson reached out and unstopped the elevator. "Five minutes tops," he interrupted.

Adrian blinked. "What?"

"That only took five minutes. Not even enough

time for people to wonder what happened." He wiped his mouth with another pristine handkerchief, then tucked it back into his suit pocket.

Adrian couldn't get his brain to work. "I have no idea what just happened." His gaze dropped to Greyson's groin, but the older man's suit jacket covered any evidence of arousal.

"You got off in the elevator," Greyson said, eyes bright. "For the second time."

I can't believe he did that. Adrian cleared his throat, still not able to think clearly. "But what about you?"

"What about me?" Greyson looked at him as the elevator stopped. The doors opened.

Adrian swallowed, hard, as the hint of arousal Greyson let show on his face made his now soft cock twitch. *And that's quite a feat, considering how hard I just got off.* He licked his lips. *What was I saying?*

"So, dinner?" Greyson asked, holding open the doors. "Tonight?"

"Yeah." Adrian nodded dumbly. How the hell could he say no to dinner after that? "Okay."

Greyson smiled. "I'll come down and get you at five o'clock sharp." He stepped out of the elevator into what looked like the plushest executive office Adrian had ever seen. Beyond the gleaming reception desk lay an open-concept expanse with views of the East River. An executive office with a glass front sat in the corner, while a conference room sat in the opposite corner. Both had incredible views of the city.

That must be Greyson's office, Adrian thought, staring out over the clean, modern space. The receptionist saw him staring and winked at him, and he flushed, eyes dropping to the company name on the front of the desk. *Dragon Investments,* he read idly, and then he stared at the words in astonishment. *Wait. Whoa.* He'd heard of them. *Everyone* had heard of them. Dragon Investments was one of the premiere venture capitalists for tech companies. Adrian's company had been trying to court them for as long as he'd worked there, to no avail, and here he was, staring at the freaking founder of the company. He had no idea they had offices in his building. *The owner of Dragon Investments just gave me head. What the actual fuck?*

"Don't be late," Greyson said. Adrian jerked his gaze from the company name just in time to see Greyson smirk at him, and then the doors shut, trapping him in the elevator by himself.

He blinked, then focused on the control panel. Greyson had managed to push the number for Adrian's floor sometime between the epic orgasm and his exit from the lift. Adrian had maybe thirty seconds to pull himself together.

"I can do this," he said to himself, straightening his shirt and pants. He picked up his laptop, still utterly discombobulated. When the doors opened, however, he grimaced. The grey carpets and cluttered desks that greeted him looked dingy compared to the pristine offices he'd just seen. Not that it mattered. He had to go to work.

"Come on, dude. Get it together." He straightened his shoulders and stepped into the chaos.

Chapter Four

Adrian rubbed his eyes. "No, Bethany. You can't tell the customer that you'll have a working prototype to demo for September. We haven't even got the user interface working yet, and I can't guarantee that we'll have it ready by then. Focus on getting me some requirements, okay?"

Bethany frowned at him. "David told me to talk to you about setting something up." She looked down at her phone. "I already called the customer, and they're free the third week of that month."

My boss is a moron, and so is Bethany, Adrian thought, but he couldn't say that out loud. David wasn't the sharpest knife in the drawer, but everyone pretended that he knew what he was talking about. And Bethany… He shook his head. She'd been driving him insane for months now. When she wasn't trying to flirt with him, she was promising impossible things and expecting him to deliver. "Look, you know as well as I do that we're running on wishes right now. I wish we had this feature, and I wish we had that other one, too, but the reality is that we're still writing the bulk of the code. We don't have a functional product yet."

Bethany sighed. "Fine." She tapped on her phone.

Adrian watched her long fingernails stab at the display with morbid fascination. He didn't even want to contemplate what it would be like sleeping with her. Everything about her was sharp. *Do straight guys actually go for women like this?*

"But you're definitely taking me out to dinner tonight. If I have to call the customer back and reschedule this demo, you owe me," she said.

Is she serious? Adrian frowned at her. "I don't owe you dinner because you messed up." He glanced at his laptop. Was it five o'clock yet? The clock in the corner of the display read four-fifty. *Dammit,* he thought, wishing he could push time forward so that he could escape this hell, but then he heard the elevator doors ding. He swung around in his chair. Greyson walked off the elevator and into the office. *Yes! Saved by the bell.* Adrian smiled and shut his laptop. "Sorry, Bethany," he said distractedly. "I'm out of here."

Greyson looked quintessentially tall, dark, and handsome walking towards him: cool, collected, and hot as fuck. Adrian shoved his computer into his bag and stood up, smiling at him. Greyson returned his grin.

Bethany frowned. "Where are you going? It's not even five yet."

Adrian rolled his eyes. "Close enough. I'm done for the day."

She grabbed his arm, digging her nails in painfully. "You're going to regret turning me down."

He shook her off. "Goodbye, Bethany." He began walking away, but then she let out a piercing scream. He flinched but didn't stop. The sooner he was gone, the better. She could have hysterics all day long for all he cared. He had a hot date that he was not about to miss.

"That's the last time, Adrian! I won't tell you no again!" Bethany shrieked.

Adrian stopped. *Shit. What the hell is she doing?* He sent Greyson an apologetic look, and then slowly turned around.

Bethany's face contorted unattractively. She'd somehow managed to smear her thick mascara, emphasizing the crazy. "How many times do I have to tell you I'm not interested, Adrian?" She rubbed her arm as if he'd grabbed her. "You think you can grab me?"

Oh, you've got to be fucking kidding me. Adrian gritted his teeth against the angry words he wanted to fling out at her.

"I didn't tell anyone about Friday night, but I'm sick of your harassment," she said, loudly enough for everyone to hear her.

"Bethany, you don't want to do this," Adrian said, keeping his voice down. Maybe he could derail the scene before she got out of hand. People had begun to stand up to see what the commotion was all about. "Trust me, you really, really don't want to do this."

"No! You can't pretend now, Adrian," she said viciously. "You got what you wanted, but now I'm going to HR to report you. I can't believe I thought you were a nice guy."

"What did he do?" one of the other women on the floor asked Bethany. A few more cast angry looks in his direction.

"I didn't do a damned thing," Adrian said, squeezing the strap of his computer bag so hard his fingers hurt. "She's making all of this up."

"That's what they all say," another woman said, stepping forward to stand with Bethany.

"He assaulted me in the elevator after work. We both stayed late, and he tried to kiss me. When I said 'No,' he pushed me into the corner and slobbered all over me," Bethany said, voice breaking. "It was awful."

Is she actually crying? Adrian thought, equal parts astonished and enraged. "Do you really think anyone is going to believe this?" he couldn't help asking. "We've never been alone in an elevator, and you know it, Bethany." He glanced around, and even some of the men were looking at him sideways now. *Fuck.*

"There's no way to prove anything. Everyone knows the elevator cameras haven't worked in ages," someone said.

"The cameras in the elevators may not work, but

the ones in the foyer do. Also, security will show exactly when everyone swiped into or out of the building." Greyson said, stepping forward. He gave Bethany a hard look. "Adrian couldn't have assaulted you because he was with me in the elevator around eight PM, and we were alone in there together during the brownout. I can vouch for him."

"Greyson." Adrian let out a relieved breath. "Hey."

Greyson smiled. "Hello, Adrian." He put a hand on Adrian's shoulder. "You ready to head out?"

"Am I ever," Adrian said. Relief made him jittery. *Or maybe that's just being so close to Greyson,* he mused as the older man leaned into him.

"You can't vouch for him," Bethany said, glaring at Greyson. "And you can't know when people enter or leave the building."

Greyson raised an eyebrow. "Oh?" He pulled out his phone and tapped the screen. "Jonah? Yes, it's Greyson. Can you check the security records for Friday during the brownout? And for several hours prior? I'm searching for a woman, named…" He tilted his head at Adrian.

"Bethany Hickson," Adrian told him.

"Bethany Hickson," Greyson repeated, still staring at her. After a moment he nodded. "You say she left at five-thirty on Friday? Interesting. Thank you, Jonah." Greyson slid his phone back into his pocket.

Bethany scowled at Greyson. "What do you think that will prove? Only security and the building owner have access to those records. You're obviously lying. You faked that phone call."

She's batshit insane, Adrian thought, too astonished to speak. Getting the security records to check her exit from the building would be a simple matter, especially if she went to Human Resources with her bullshit accusation. He saw a few of the others on the floor frowning as they looked at her. *Yeah, think it through, idiots. Bethany is a liar.*

Greyson smiled coldly. "My dear, I *am* the building owner." He slid a business card out of his pocket and held it out. "Moreover, Adrian isn't interested in you, or any women, because he's *my* boyfriend, and I can assure you, he is definitely not straight." He gave her a hard look. "Also, I *will* be talking to your company's HR department about your behavior. They won't want to find out that their lease is in jeopardy because one of their employees can't take no for an answer." He tilted his head. "You do realize that your harassment of Adrian is a firing offense?"

"Uh," Adrian said, then shut up. He didn't care if he was outed. After all, the only reason he'd kept it quiet was to avoid discussing his personal life at work. Greyson cocked his head at him, but Adrian shook his head. "Never mind."

Bethany snatched the card from Greyson. "This building is owned by Dragon Investment Group, Mr. Whoever-You-Are, and I don't think the owner of *that* particular company will appreciate you impersonating—" She stopped abruptly, staring at the card in her hand. "Wait. This can't be right," she muttered as she glanced up at Greyson and paled.

Greyson snorted. "I see you've finally put two and two together." He turned to Adrian. "There's a reason I've been avoiding working with your company."

Adrian nodded, thinking of all the missed project deadlines. "Yeah, I've been thinking of looking for a different job."

"You have?" Greyson smiled. "I know just the place for you. I need a technical director who knows his way around the business to advise us."

Adrian flushed at the look in Greyson's eyes. "Let's get through dinner before we do anything drastic, okay?" He rolled his shoulders to try to dispel the tension of the last few minutes.

"Wait, are you telling me that you're dating Greyson Lee? Greyson Lee from Dragon Investments?" Bethany asked, voice rising. Her expression was a strange combination of horror and admiration. "Since when are you gay?"

"Since always," Adrian said, exasperated. "I told you I wasn't interested, Bethany. You didn't listen."

She glanced around, scowling when she realized that she'd lost her sympathetic audience. "Just because you're gay doesn't mean you didn't assault me," she told Adrian.

Adrian rolled his eyes so hard he was surprised they didn't pop out of his head. He was done with this situation. Beyond done. "Give it up, Bethany. You know I didn't assault you. Security has you clocking out right in the middle of rush hour, long before I left. There is no way we would've been alone on an elevator together at five o'clock, and everyone knows it."

Bethany opened her mouth, but Greyson cut her off before she could speak.

"Think very carefully before you speak, Ms. Hickson. I can have you escorted off the property," he said.

Adrian nodded. "And I will be filing a complaint about your false accusation, as well as the other times you harassed me."

Bethany looked from Adrian to Greyson and back again, face closing down. "I hope you two are very happy together," she spat, then flounced away.

"She'll be gone by the end of this week,"

Greyson said.

Adrian raised his brows. "You think?" He wasn't quite as certain as Greyson that Bethany would suffer the consequences of her behavior. He knew his company's track record about such things wasn't great.

Greyson snorted. "I *know*. As soon as I call her supervisor, it will happen."

"Oh. Well, that's … huh." Adrian said, shaking his head. "That was a hell of a thing."

"That was not quite the thing I was hoping for," Greyson said dryly.

Adrian laughed as he turned to his boyfriend. "Exactly what thing were you hoping for?"

"This thing." Greyson tugged him closer and kissed him lightly on the lips, in full view of everyone. "And I'd like to try out some other things. More things." He paused, then smirked. "But not here."

Adrian laughed. "And not in the elevator, right?"

"Hmm." Greyson tilted his head as he half-smiled. "We'll see."

Chapter Five

"Whoa. This place is swanky," Adrian said, running a hand over the beautiful woodwork in Greyson's private elevator. They'd finished dinner at a delicious Korean restaurant, and then Greyson had invited Adrian back to his penthouse. Since his apartment building sat near Central Park, Adrian assumed the views would be incredible. He was looking forward to lounging in a real bed with Mr. Hottie. He grinned, feeling like the cat that got the canary. He'd even managed to give Greyson back his button without acting like a complete fool. They'd laughed about it over dessert. All in all, his life was looking up.

Greyson shrugged. "It's home." He smiled at Adrian, and then just as the elevator stopped at the top floor, he hit the emergency button, keeping the doors shut.

Adrian blinked. "What are you doing? I thought we were going to have some coffee?" He laughed a little under his breath. Everyone knew that "coffee" was a euphemism for hooking up.

"You seem to like my elevator," Greyson said, crowding him up against the wall.

Adrian opened his mouth, but then Greyson kissed him, and all thoughts of protest disappeared. "Oh, fuck me," he muttered when the older man let him up for air a few minutes later. He was hard as hell, and desperate for relief. "How do you do this to me? You gave me a fantastic blowjob only this morning."

Greyson chuckled, but instead of answering, he was busy undoing Adrian's clothes. "Off with this."

"Wait, seriously?" Adrian helped him with his shirt, but then Greyson started on his pants. "But we're in an elevator." He glanced around. No security cameras in here that he could see, but the polished doors showed his frazzled look quite clearly. He frowned at himself even as Greyson messed with his pants. He almost didn't recognize the man staring back at him. Shouldn't he feel more anxious about this?

"It's my private elevator," Greyson said, shoving down Adrian's slacks. "And I want to fuck you right here. Right now."

Adrian swallowed, still staring at his reflection. It showed him just how far gone he looked: hair a mess, mouth swollen, and his cock standing straight out, begging for attention. "Don't you have a bed?" he managed to ask.

"Yes, and you'll see it." Greyson tore off his shirt and kicked his shoes into the corner. "Later." He went to his knees again.

"Oh God." Adrian scrabbled at the walls as Greyson sucked his cock down his throat. Before he could get off, the older man stopped, fingers trailing back behind his balls. Somehow, he'd managed to find lube, because when he began to finger Adrian's ass, he slipped right in. "Holy fuck," Adrian stuttered, hips jerking.

"That's it. Let me in," Greyson said, smiling up at him. He slipped another finger in, then crooked it, hitting Adrian's prostate.

Adrian moaned as he stared down at Greyson's dark eyes. He could barely keep himself from screwing down on the older man's hand. "Please. Don't stop." He licked his lips. "This is nuts."

Greyson laughed and stood up, ignoring Adrian's protest. He had a condom in his hand. "Over here."

Adrian could barely stand, let alone walk. Greyson urged him toward the doors. "Palms on the brass." He lifted Adrian's hands until they were pressed on the cool metal. "That's it. That's perfect."

This might work, but only because he's built like a fucking brick house. Adrian watched Greyson's reflection as the older man put on the condom. "You're crazy."

"You love it," Greyson said, kissing his shoulder. "You ready?"

Adrian nodded. "Come on." His throbbing erection brushed against the cool doors. He trembled. They were going to leave a mess.

Greyson moved closer, nudging between his ass cheeks. "You're so fucking hot, Adrian."

Adrian shivered. Greyson had his teeth on his shoulders, and the sting made everything a thousand times better. "Come on, old man."

"Who you calling old?" Greyson bent his knees and pushed his cock right up against Adrian's hole. "I'm not too old to do this," he said, and pushed inside.

Adrian groaned, loving the burn. "Oh, shit." He wasn't sure he could remain standing. He sucked in air, trying to relax. "I'm not going to make it," he gasped as Greyson surged into his body.

"Breathe." Greyson held still, panting into Adrian's neck.

"Fuck." Adrian let his eyes close as his forehead pressed into the brass.

"No, look at me," Greyson said roughly.

Adrian forced his eyes open. "Fucking move. Please."

Greyson's eyes darkened, and then he was pulling out.

"No," Adrian said through gritted teeth, but Greyson just smiled and shoved back in, screwing him into the door. "Jesus, Greyson. You're a beast."

"You know it." Greyson said, thrusting again, and then again. "You like this, don't you?"

Adrian nodded, completely unable to form words. His cock slapped against the metal with every thrust. He couldn't tell if he was going to come or pass out.

Greyson bared his teeth and moved faster, hands on Adrian's hips. "Take it. You can take it."

Adrian stared at Greyson's face, distorted by the brass, and knew he was never, ever going to want anyone as much as he wanted this man. "Come on. Harder, Greyson," he managed to say, and Greyson growled and shoved into him so hard he went onto his toes. His cock was pressed against the door, and he was nearly there. "Come on."

Greyson bit into his shoulder, then slipped his hand around to grip Adrian's erection, hard and rough. Adrian lost it. His climax rushed through him, from his head to his toes, in a giant, hot rush, and he cried out as semen splashed over Greyson's hand and onto the doors.

"Fuck, you're gorgeous," Greyson said, and then he groaned long and low.

Adrian felt the older man's cock swell and then jerk as he orgasmed. Greyson slumped down against Adrian, and they slid down the door into a heap on the floor.

It was a long time before Adrian could move, and when he finally pried his eyes open, he laughed. The brass doors were smeared with his jizz. It looked like someone had spilled glue all over the shiny metal and then rubbed it in. He touched it with a finger and grimaced. It was already drying.

"What?" Greyson grumbled. He shifted them until they were both sitting bare assed on the floor.

Adrian pointed at the door. "That's going to be a bitch to clean up."

Greyson laughed. "No worries. I have people for that."

Flushing, Adrian shook his head as he imagined some poor cleaner having to deal with his semen. He made a mental note to wipe it up later, if he could. "Of course you do," he said, wincing as his sit bones protested. He was only twenty-five and he was too old for this shit. *Even if it is kind of kinky,* he thought, kissing Greyson fondly. The older man looked as wrecked as he felt. "So, where's that bed you promised me?"

Greyson kissed him back, sliding his hand into Adrian's hair. "You can have a hell of a lot more than my bed, Adrian. You know that, right?" His voice was low and serious.

Adrian went still. "What are you saying?"

"I'm saying I think I'm falling in love with you."

Adrian stared at Greyson, then reached up and brushed the older man's messy hair out of his face. "Good." His voice cracked. He'd dreamed of someone saying those words to him, but he'd never really believed it would happen.

"Good? That's all you have to say?" Greyson's eyes twinkled.

Adrian nodded. He would *not* fucking cry. "Yeah, because I think I'm going to need a new job soon, and you have connections," he said, trying to ignore the way his heart pounded.

Greyson laughed. "I do."

"And I'm going to shamelessly use you for those connections, because you're my boyfriend," Adrian said, feeling happier than he could ever remember. *Is this what love feels like?* he wondered, touching Greyson's lips. The man had the most luscious mouth on the planet.

"Oh? Exactly how shameless are you?" Greyson asked, lips moving against Adrian's fingertips. Amusement colored his voice.

"We just fucked in an elevator," Adrian replied

dryly. "I think you know the answer to that, Mr. Hottie."

"But will you fuck on the balcony?" Greyson asked, standing up. He held out his hand.

Adrian stared up at him. If he took the hand Greyson offered, he knew his life would never be the same. Slowly he reached out. Greyson's hand was warm and infinitely steady. "For you, I'll fuck anywhere." He stood up and pressed his lips to Greyson's, putting everything he felt but couldn't say out loud into his kiss: *Don't ever let me go, because I think I love you.*

Greyson kissed him softly, and then he pushed the button on the elevator. The doors opened, and he dropped his arm over Adrian's shoulders. "Come on. The bed is this way."

Adrian took a deep breath and walked into the future with Greyson.

The End

THE CABIN

Close Proximity, 2

Erin M. Leaf

Copyright © 2018

Chapter One

The tall, black man who'd entered just before him stood at least six feet tall, and was built like a bouncer, but he wore the glasses of an artist. The dichotomy intrigued him, but Flynn Russell was too tired to puzzle out why, even as he watched the guy frown at the girl behind the desk. Flynn rubbed his face while he waited for his key, wishing he'd at least stopped to change his tux before showing up here like a homeless person. In his formal attire and winter coat, he looked as out of place at this rustic wilderness resort as the black guy arguing with the clerk. Mostly older couples came here, and sometimes families, but rarely did they arrive at the tail end of October, in the middle of an early winter storm.

Yet here I am, Flynn thought, wondering once again if he'd done the right thing in coming.

"I'm so sorry, Mr. Green, but somehow the reservation system messed up your arrival date. You're in the system for next year on this date," the girl said, looking beyond flustered as the large man stared down at her.

"Miss, it's sleeting out there. And my ride is already gone. If you can't find a place for me, I'm going to be camping out in your lobby here until the weather clears." The man gestured around the small rustic space. The small dreads that topped off his perfectly shaped side-fade didn't move as he spoke. His deep voice was surprisingly soft for a man of his size.

"Cabin ninety-three is booked out to a newlywed couple, and the others have already been winterized, and have no running water or bedding," the girl said, tapping a finger on the tablet in front of her. "I don't know what to do." She glanced around as if a solution was going to jump out at her from the log walls.

Wait. Newlywed couple? Flynn's gut twisted, and he grimaced. Given the location and the time of year, odds were, she was talking about him. *And the wife I'm supposed to be here with. Fuck.*

The large man sighed. "You realize no plane will fly in this?" He glanced out of the large window near the door. "And there's no way I could even get a ride to the airport at this hour, especially since it's a two-hour drive away."

Flynn set his bag down. He'd barely managed to get here himself, and he had an all-wheel drive crossover vehicle. He stepped forward. "Let me guess. Cabin ninety-three is for Flynn and Darlene Russell, right?"

The girl looked at him with a hint of panic in her gaze. "Yes." She took in his tuxedo and bit her lip. "Oh no."

"Oh yes." Flynn nodded grimly, already reaching

for his wallet. "That would be me." He held out his identification. He looked at the black guy, not surprised to find resignation in the man's expression. This was a fucked-up situation, no doubt about it.

The girl took his driver's license and glanced down at it, then handed it back. "The cabin is all ready for you, Mr. Russell." She attempted a smile, which faded as she realized there was no Mrs. Russell with him. "Is your wife in your car?"

Flynn ignored the shame twisting down his spine. It wasn't *his* fault that Darlene had jilted him at the altar. "I'm not actually married," he said shortly, not wanting to get into the whole debacle. He could still see the dismay on his mother's face as Darlene bolted out of the church. The entire, nasty disaster had played on repeat in his brain in full Technicolor over and over again during the entire drive up through New Hampshire. He hoped his mom and dad had made it back home to Pittsburgh. The only reason he'd agreed to get married in Boston was because Darlene's parents lived there. He glanced at the poor dude in front of him and sighed. There was no reason to toss the guy out in the cold, especially when he knew his cabin had a sofa as well as a bed. "You can stay with me." He looked outside. "At least until the storm lets up."

The man stepped back, looking over Flynn's tux. "That's not necessary." His gaze lingered on Flynn's undone bowtie. "I'm sure you don't want me crowding in with you."

Flynn gave a short laugh, knowing exactly what the guy meant. *He's wondering about the absent Mrs. Russell. Join the club*, he thought derisively. "It's just me. I didn't actually get married today." He took off his coat. It was hot as hell in here suddenly. "Sometimes things don't go as planned," he explained.

The man's expression eased into sympathy, just what Flynn wanted to avoid. "I'm sorry." Clearly the man knew there was story there.

Flynn shook his head. "Not your fault. Hell, it's not *my* fault." He raked his hand through his hair and turned back to the girl. "Give me two keys."

She looked from him to the other guy and back again. "Are you sure?" She glanced out the window and made a face. "He's right about the airports. I'm heading for home as soon as I check you in here."

Flynn nodded. "I'm sure." How bad could it be? The guy didn't look like a psycho, and Flynn was easygoing enough to get along with almost anyone. That's why his father always made him deal with the more difficult customers at their automotive shop.

"I appreciate it. And of course I'll pay you for half the cost of the reservation," the big guy said quietly.

Flynn waved a hand. He didn't even care about that. "No worries, Mr...." He trailed off, tilting his head expectantly.

"Beauregard Green," the guy said, holding out a hand. "Call me Beau."

Flynn shook it, absently admiring the collection of wood beaded and leather bracelets the man wore. Flynn didn't wear much jewelry because it wasn't safe in the shop, but he could appreciate it on other people. The man's grip was firm, but not crushing. He'd dealt with enough egotistical pricks who tried to crush his knuckles to appreciate a normal handshake. It wasn't that Flynn was weak, far from it. You couldn't do custom car fabrication without putting some muscle into the job, but he spent a lot of his time trying to get along with difficult rich people. This guy's quiet confidence was definitely scoring points with him. "Flynn Russell. Nice to meet you."

The girl slid her tablet into a drawer and held out two keys to him. "Are you certain you want to do this?" she asked, eyeing Beau as if he ate small children for breakfast.

Flynn barely refrained from rolling his eyes. The girl probably didn't see a lot of minorities up here in the middle of the New England woods, but that was no excuse for her weirdness. "I'm positive," he said.

She nodded and dropped the keys into his palm, then handed him a pamphlet. "This details what to do in case of an emergency." She glanced outside again and grimaced. "Power outage and stuff." She handed him another paper. "Here's a map. Your cabin is up the hill and in the pine grove." She pointed to a small icon she'd circled in red. "I hope your car can make it up the road."

"I'll be fine." Flynn took both papers and tucked them into his pocket, then shrugged his coat back on. It didn't match his tux, but who would care? It wasn't like he was trying to impress anyone anymore. "Come on. My car's out front," he said to Beau.

Beau nodded and picked up his duffel.

"That all you got?" Flynn asked.

"Yup. This was supposed to be a relaxing retreat." He smiled wryly. "My dad confiscated my camera, but I managed to hide a drawing pad from him. And he couldn't take my phone, so I'll still be able to take a few pictures."

"No reception up here, though," Flynn said.

Beau made a face. "True."

Flynn held open the door for him. "Camera? Are you a photographer, then?"

"I'm more artist than photographer, though some people would argue that point," Beau replied, flinching as the sleet hit his face. "Damn. I forgot how much this kind of weather sucks." He shook his head. "I'm getting soft living in LA."

"LA is a hell of a long way to travel for sleet," Flynn said, unlocking his car door. "Throw your duffel in the back."

Beau did as he said, and then slid in the passenger's seat. "Nice car."

Flynn had to laugh at that. *He* liked his Subaru, but, compared to the BMWs and other luxury cars he'd worked on, it was nothing special. "It's a good crossover vehicle, and it's fantastic in bad weather. I have a truck back home that my dad and I share." He shrugged. "This car isn't fancy, but it gets me where I need to go." He eased on the gas, pleased that the sleet hadn't yet frozen to the windshield. He pulled away from the main cabin and drove for a minute before turning right onto a gravel road. His car had no trouble dealing with the ruts in the road, and he smiled grimly. *At least my car never lets me down.*

"Sometimes the fancy things are all show and no function," Beau said, patting the dash. "This car is beautiful because it does what it's designed to do perfectly."

True words, Flynn thought, struck by the simple statement. Did that mean his ex-fiancée had been nothing more than a fancy facade? But a facade for what? And was their relationship all for show? He grimaced as he glanced over at his passenger. "That's an unusual sentiment."

Beau grinned. "It's an artist thing. I was trained in design, and form always follows function."

"Makes sense." Flynn navigated around a curve, following the dirt road up the ridge line. Every so often they had to drive over erosion bumps. After five more minutes of driving, they hadn't gotten to the cabin yet.

"Where in the world is this place?" Beau asked,

staring out the window. The sleet had begun to coat the last of the autumn leaves, leaving the forest looking like someone had thrown sugar at a bowl of colorful cereal.

"It's the most private cabin," Flynn replied. "It should be just around here." He nodded as the oaks and maples gave way to eastern pine and hemlock. "There it is." He drove up to a small cabin and parked in front.

"Seems a strange place for a honeymoon," Beau murmured, getting out of the car. He held a hand over his eyes as the wind whipped sleet into his face again.

"Come on, get your stuff," Flynn said, not answering the man's unspoken question. He'd always loved going camping and hiking. Darlene hadn't, but she'd agreed to do a split honeymoon: one week here, and one week in Vegas later in the year, during the Christmas holidays. He snorted as he grabbed his backpack and bag. At least they hadn't yet booked the Vegas trip. He followed Beau up the path to the front door, and let the taller man unlock it.

"Whoa," Beau said as he stepped inside.

"You were expecting a hovel, weren't you?" Flynn asked, amused. He kicked the door shut and took in the space. The tile floor at the entryway extended into the kitchen where stainless-steel appliances gleamed in the low lighting. The tile turned to hardwood where the living room began. A large leather sofa sat in front of a huge fireplace. He knew from when he'd booked the place that the bedroom was to the left, along with the bathroom. "It's the largest of their cabins."

"The one I rented was a studio," Beau said, eyebrows raised. "This place is amazing."

"Well, it was *supposed* to be my honeymoon," Flynn said, sighing. Exhaustion was hitting him hard. Or was it disillusionment? "I'm going to dump my stuff in the bedroom."

"I'll sleep on the sofa," Beau said, heading towards it.

Flynn nodded. The damn thing was big enough to sleep three men of Beau's size.

After he'd unpacked, he wandered back out to the living space. Beau was in the kitchen, staring into the refrigerator. "There's lasagna in here," he said, sounding surprised.

"Yeah. I had meals prepped as part of the package," Flynn said.

Beau looked up, then blinked. "You're still wearing your tux."

Flynn shrugged. "I'm going to sleep as soon as I eat. Seemed a waste of energy to change." He nodded at the fridge. "Get out the lasagna. Might as well drown my woes in pasta."

Beau nodded and pulled out the casserole. "We can heat it in the microwave. It says it's fully cooked."

Flynn nodded and sat down at the kitchen island. The cabin was large, as cabins went, but it lacked a dining room. He didn't think it would matter when he'd made the reservations. *Fuck. This is stupid. Why did I come here?* he wondered, rubbing his face. The microwave binged, dragging him out of his spiraling funk.

"Why didn't you just cancel the reservation?" Beau asked, sitting down with the steaming lasagna.

Flynn sighed. "Because I'm an idiot?"

Beau looked at him steadily. "Are you?"

That's a hell of a stare this guy's got, Flynn thought, slightly unnerved. "Eh. Who knows?" He took the plate Beau offered him and spooned some pasta onto it. "I guess I should explain, huh?"

Beau pursed his lips. "You don't have to."

Why does this guy make me feel so unsettled? The

sympathy in his gaze freaked Flynn out. "Let me just get it out, and then we can not talk about it for the rest of the night, okay?"

Beau lifted an eyebrow, but he nodded. "Sure." He leaned back in his chair.

Flynn took a deep breath. "Darlene and I dated for two years. We got along. She was nice. I asked her to marry me. She said yes." He stopped to push some of the pasta around his plate. "I thought everything was fine, and then, right before she was supposed to walk down the aisle, she stopped, and ran off crying." He swallowed the annoyance rising his throat and pushed the plate away. "I went after her, and she told me she couldn't go through with it."

"Did she say why?"

Flynn gritted his teeth. "She said there was no spark. She said we were great friends, but she could tell I didn't really want her." He set his fork down with a clatter. "I have no idea where she got that idea, but that was it. My mother cried. Darlene left. I left. The guests left. The end."

Beau rubbed his chin. "That's terrible."

"Yeah." Flynn nodded, then dragged the plate back over and began eating. "I was upset." He chewed and swallowed. "The thing is…" He trailed off.

Was he really going to say this out loud? He looked at Beau. His whiskey brown eyes looked at Flynn without even an iota of judgment. *Fuck it. He's a total stranger, but he's clearly not an asshole. And he's a good listener.* "The thing is, I wasn't all that disappointed. I was more upset because my mother was upset." Flynn shook his head. "That's fucked up." He stared out the window over the sink. "I don't even really miss her. That just isn't normal."

Beau didn't say anything for a long moment. "So,

your ex was right."

Flynn flinched. "No." He took another bite of lasagna, chewed it, and swallowed. "Maybe." He set his fork down. "I don't know what's wrong with me. Darlene is a nice person. We got along just fine."

Beau tilted his head. "I'm going to go out on a limb here."

"Okay." Flynn waited, but Beau didn't speak. He looked at Flynn, and then looked away. Outside, sleet scoured at the windows.

"Just say it. I'm not going to freak out." Flynn laughed. "I'm not that kind of guy. I'm actually really easygoing. Always have been."

"You sure about that?" Beau half smiled as he turned his head back to Flynn, but before Flynn could reply, he continued, "You ever think that maybe you tried to fall in love with the wrong person?"

Flynn frowned. "I have no idea what you mean."

"You always date girls?" Beau asked.

"Do I always date—" Flynn snapped his mouth shut. *He's asking if I'm dating on the wrong side of the fence. Shit.* He stared at Beau.

Beau held his gaze for a moment, and then began calmly eating his lasagna as if he hadn't just dropped a bomb into Flynn's lap.

Chapter Two

Flynn stared at Beau's ass as he draped the extra blanket over the sofa. The man was built like a truck: solid and strong. He shook his head. Since when did he check out other guys' butts? *Since Beau asked me if I've ever dated one,* he told himself, flushing at the thought. Beau moved all the decorative pillows to one end of the sofa while Flynn chewed over what to say. Did he really have to say anything? Could a person die from embarrassment? The questions circling his mind were driving him nuts.

"You look like a man with a lot on his mind," Beau said, taking off his shoes.

"No. I never dated a guy," Flynn finally offered, letting the words drop awkwardly into the silence. They'd finished their dinner without talking because Flynn, completely derailed by Beau's question, couldn't think of a damned thing to say. Beau didn't speak either, probably because he was afraid Flynn would freak out if he said anything else. *Of course, I'm not the kind of guy who flies off the handle for no good reason,* Flynn reminded himself. Truthfully, it hadn't even occurred to him to let loose on Beau. Flynn wasn't angry. Just surprised. And confused. "Do I look like I'm gay?" he asked, almost afraid of the answer.

Beau looked up and snorted. "Do *I* look like I'm gay?"

Flynn looked at the man's small dreads, and the glasses he'd tucked into the neck of his blue shirt. *He looks like an artist.* Flynn shook his head. "No. Of course not."

Beau nodded. "There you go. Appearances don't mean nothing, my Pop always said."

Flynn nodded. That was that, then. End of

discussion.

"Because I've been gay my whole life," Beau continued, opening his duffel and extracting a pair of sweats and a t-shirt as if he hadn't said anything important. "It's not like us homos go around wearing little rainbow flag pins." He grinned. "Well, not all the time."

Flynn froze. "Wait. What?"

Beau looked at him, one eyebrow cocked. "You heard me."

Flynn licked suddenly dry lips. "Oh."

Beau chuckled. "You look like you just swallowed a rock." He pursed his lips. "Or a bird, and it's flitting around in there." He gestured to Flynn's stomach. "That's got to be uncomfortable."

How can he joke about this? Flynn forced himself to act normal. He walked over to the fireplace and crouched down to check the flue. "I had no idea." He shoved open the mesh curtains hung across the opening and twisted down to peer up into the chimney. His lower back protested the awkward position, but he ignored it.

"I know you didn't," Beau said.

What the hell is that supposed to mean? Flynn looked over at Beau, neck still craned uncomfortably. "Are you making a point about my observational skills?" He reached into the fireplace and tugged on the flue's lever. A puff of soot blew up into his face, and he coughed. "Shit."

"I'm just saying that you seem strangely chill for a dude who was just stood up at the altar." Beau walked over and nudged Flynn's knee with his foot.

Flynn extricated himself, squatting in front of the hearth. "I don't know what you're talking about."

Beau handed him a wad of newspaper. "You went on your honeymoon. Alone." He shook his head as Flynn tossed the paper onto the grate in the fireplace.

"I like being in the woods," Flynn replied, not sure what Beau was getting at.

"Light the fire," Beau said, holding out a handful of kindling.

Flynn took it and placed it on top of the newspaper. "I don't have a match."

Solemnly, Beau stuck his hand into his jeans pocket and pulled out a book of matches.

Flynn watched him, eyes unwillingly drawn to Beau's groin. The bulge there looked fairly substantial. He tore his gaze away. "Are you messing with me?"

Beau's expression lightened. "What? No." He held out the matches. "Take them."

Flynn gingerly accepted the matches. The book had the name of a bar printed across the top in rainbow colors. "I'm assuming this is a gay bar," he muttered, suddenly amused. "Is this the equivalent of a rainbow pin?"

Beau laughed. "Just light the fire, man."

Flynn shook his head. Weirdly, he felt better than he had since Darlene had fled the scene of the crime. He lit the newspaper, then tossed a few medium sized pieces of wood on top of the kindling. Fortunately, the bin near the fireplace had a huge amount of dry wood. If they lost power, they'd at least stay warm.

"So," Beau said, when Flynn stood up.

"So," Flynn replied, dusting his hands on his tux. It was a rental, but he really didn't give a shit right now. Beau was looking at him speculatively. "What?" He glanced down at his legs and grimaced. He'd really made a mess of his slacks.

"Go change into something less weird. I can't look at you in that thing. It's all *March of the Penguins* in here. We can play cards or whatever, since I don't see a television in this place."

March of the Penguins? Ha. Flynn grinned. "I don't look weird. I look good in a tux." He struck a pose. "See? Even jilted, I'm a sharp dressed man."

Beau's eyes flashed with something Flynn didn't recognize for a moment, and then he smiled. "Go change, white boy, before you trip over your ego."

Flynn laughed and headed to the bedroom.

****

"That's it. You officially suck," Beau said, tossing his cards down. He took off his little glasses and tossed them after the cards.

Does he even need those things? Flynn wondered as he rubbed his hands together mock gleefully. "I rock at gin rummy."

"You rock at being a total dork," Beau responded instantly. "We should've played poker."

"I suck at poker," Flynn said, gathering up the deck.

"Of course you do." Beau stood up and stretched.

Flynn watched the man lift his arms over his head and twist his back. A few cards slipped out of his hands as his fingers went lax. "Jesus. How much do you work out?" Flynn asked. Even with the loose t-shirt he could see muscles stacked on top of muscles. Flynn hit the gym a couple times a week and he knew he was strong, but he'd never looked like that.

Beau glanced over his shoulder. "Genetics. I take after my Pop."

"Even genetics won't give you that kind of body if you don't work for it." Flynn grabbed the cards he'd dropped. Why did Beau's body bother him so much? It wasn't as if he'd never seen another guy's torso before. Hell, he looked at one every day in the bathroom mirror. *Stop staring, or he'll pound you,* he told himself. The last thing he needed after the hell of this day was to piss off his unexpected roommate.

"I like to work out. Relieves tension," Beau said, sitting back down. He cocked his head. "You work out, too." He poked at Flynn's biceps.

Flynn faked a wince, rubbing his arm. "Yeah, I do. So what?"

Beau smirked. "You realize straight guys don't sit around talking about their muscles with each other."

"Yes, they do," Flynn said, frowning. "I've talked about lifting with guys before."

"You're not talking about lifting. You're talking about how I look," Beau said, eyes narrowing.

Is Beau right? Flynn stared at the larger man, then looked away. "Shit. I'm just tired. Ignore me." He finished stacking the cards and was putting them in their case, when the lights flickered and went out, plunging the room into darkness. The only light left came from the fire. "Ah, hell." He tossed the cards onto the coffee table.

"That means our heat just went, doesn't it?" Beau stood up and went to poke at the breaker box set into the wall near the fireplace. "Yup. The fuses are all fine. Power is out."

"Damn." Flynn rubbed his face. He was toasty warm here in front of the fireplace, but he knew he'd be cold soon enough when he went to sleep in the bedroom. "Why would they use electric heat up here?"

"Because this is mostly a summer resort, and they don't really plan for blizzards," Beau said, sitting back down. "You can't sleep in there." He nodded towards the bedroom.

Flynn shrugged. "I'll be all right."

Beau shook his head. "Yeah, sure. For about two hours. And then you'll be a Popsicle."

That startled a laugh out of Flynn. "A little

pessimistic, are we?"

"Dude. I grew up in northwest PA, near Erie. You ever hear of lake effect snow?" Beau stood up again and started lighting the candles set on top of the mantle.

"I grew up in Pittsburgh," Flynn said, watching him move a few candles from the mantle to the coffee table. "Still live there, actually."

Beau glanced at him. "I went to school there. Art major."

Flynn wasn't surprised. "Pitt?"

"CMU." Beau didn't elaborate, but then, he didn't have to. Everyone knew that CMU meant Carnegie Mellon University, and that it had a fantastic art program.

"That's a hell of a tough school to get into." His estimation of Beau's intelligence went up even further. "I went to Pitt. Business major."

Beau nodded. "Makes sense, since you said something about a shop."

"Yeah, me and my dad own the business together. We do custom work for high end cars." He yawned. "I should go." He jerked his thumb over his shoulder.

"Don't." Beau put a hand on his wrist. "I'm serious. You'll freeze in there. Too many windows and no insulation will make for a very uncomfortable night."

Flynn went perfectly still as his heart gave a nasty thump against his ribs. What the hell was wrong with him? His cock started to swell, and he panicked, standing up. "I gotta take a—" He clamped his mouth shut and fled to the bathroom.

Once inside, he closed the door, and then realized he could barely see. "Shit," he said, glaring at the outline of his reflection. He could just make out the shape of his head. "What the hell is wrong with you?" He hadn't been this jumpy on his first date with Darlene. He adjusted his cock. Was it because the guy had told him he was gay? Was he having some kind of weird, homophobic reaction? A knock on the door made him jump.

"Flynn, open up. I brought you the lamp from the kitchen. You're not going to be able to see the toilet in there," Beau called. "You don't want to piss on your feet, do you?"

Flynn gripped the edge of the sink so hard his knuckles ached. "Okay." He cleared his throat and tried again. "Hang on." He made his way to the door and opened it. Beau stood just outside with the LED light illuminating his smooth, dark skin. His eyes glowed in the light. Flynn felt like Beau could see right into his soul, and he looked down as he reached out. That didn't help, because now all he could see were the muscles stretching up Beau's forearm.

Beau held out the light. "Man, you've gotta chill out. You're wound tighter than a two-dollar watch."

Flynn took the lantern. Their fingers brushed, and he almost winced when his cock went from hard to painful. "Thanks."

Beau nodded and backed away.

Flynn shut the door and set the lamp on the counter. Then he pushed down his sweats and took his dick in his hand. Beau's face, lit by firelight, popped into his mind, and he groaned, hand already stroking. "This is wrong," he muttered at his reflection. His cock didn't care. He grimaced and tried to picture Darlene's face. It didn't work. He couldn't even remember if her eyes were blue or green. "What the hell is wrong with you?" he whispered, remembering the way Beau's leather bracelets hugged his wrists. What would it feel like if Beau were the one stroking him, instead of himself?

That was it. His cock jerked, and he huffed out a breath as an orgasm came out of nowhere. He gripped his erection, hard, but he couldn't stop it any more than he could stop a freight train coming in. Jizz coated his hand, and he bent over, shuddering. Beau had an amazing face: strong cheekbones, a short beard, and the hint of a scar just under his right eye. Flynn wanted to touch it and see if it was real. He shuddered again as his cock throbbed with the aftermath of one of the strongest orgasms of his life.

A long minute later he turned on the faucet, grateful that there was enough heat left in the hot water heater for him to wash up. "You're losing it," he told himself harshly when he'd finished and tucked himself back in. He stared at the door, then sighed. Time to face the music.

Chapter Three

"So, how'd you meet your ex?" Beau asked.

Flynn tensed, then made himself relax. They were at opposite ends of the sofa with their feet tangled up. The damned thing was almost big enough for them to sleep without touching. *Almost, but not quite,* Flynn mused, trying not to let on how freaked out he was over Beau's feet warming his own. He was freaked out because he *liked* it, not because he was an asshole. He was freaked out because he should be upset over his failed wedding, but instead, he was feeling almost relieved. *What does that say about me?* he wondered. He looked down the length of the couch to find Beau watching him with an indecipherable expression on his face. "She came in to pick up a car for her brother that we'd customized. I asked her out. She said yes."

Beau hmm'd. The fire crackled, and a log crashed down, sending sparks flying out.

"What?" Flynn asked, defensive. "We got along. She was nice."

"You keep saying 'nice' like it's a good reason to hook up with someone," Beau said. He shifted on the sofa, bumping Flynn's ankles with his toes. "It's not. You should only date someone if there's a spark there."

Flynn scowled, knowing Beau couldn't see his expression. "Have you ever felt that way?" He had no idea if the guy had a boyfriend or what.

Beau nodded. "I have. Once." He smiled, teeth white in the darkness. "He was my first love. We were in high school, and neither of us knew what the hell we were doing." He sighed. "That was a long time ago."

"I don't even know how old you are," Flynn said.

"Thirty. High school was a long time ago."

"I'm twenty-six," Flynn said, feeling much

younger than Beau, for some reason. *But I'm not really. It's just ... he really seems to have his shit together, unlike me.*

"You've got time, then," Beau told him, as if he could read Flynn's mind.

"Time for what?" Flynn had a feeling he knew what the man was getting at, but he wanted to hear the words.

"Time to fall in love." Beau lifted his arms and tucked them behind his head. All that did was showcase his ridiculous physique. "That girl you were engaged to didn't do it for you. I'm surprised no one said something to you about it."

Flynn tore his eyes away from the man's biceps and focused on the fire. His damned cock felt super-sensitive. *What the hell? I literally just got off half an hour ago. And also, I was supposed to be married to a woman just this morning. My dick is broken.* He scowled at his groin. "My dad told me it wasn't going to work out, but I didn't believe him." He fidgeted uncomfortably as his erection rubbed against his sweatpants. "My mom was really excited about it, though."

Beau laughed. "I imagine that's a mom thing."

Flynn nodded. "Yeah."

"My pop told me that someday I'd meet a girl, and nothing would ever be the same. Imagine his surprise when he found out I'd met a boy, instead," Beau said.

"He didn't approve? That sucks." Flynn wasn't surprised. A lot of parents were not at all cool with their kid being gay.

"Approve? Ha. No. He did not." Beau shifted his weight again, bringing his arms down. "It was a dark time, my man. A very dark time."

"Did you eventually make peace with him?" Flynn knew his dad would be fine with him dating a guy.

His mom? He wasn't sure about her, but he had a feeling that if she was unhappy with the idea, it would only be because she wanted grandkids.

"We did," Beau said. "It took a long time, and a lot of angry words, but then he met his new wife. My stepmom helped a lot."

"That's unusual," Flynn said. He couldn't even imagine his parents married to someone else.

"Yeah, but that's her style. Andrea don't take no shit from no man." Beau laughed as he slipped into vernacular to describe his stepmother. "I like her. And now I have five-year-old twin brothers. They're awesome."

"Sounds great," Flynn said, distracted by the way Beau was playing with his bracelets. "What about your mom? Did she have a problem with it?"

"My mother died right after I was born. She had a stroke."

Oh, hell. Way to put your foot in it, Flynn. "I'm so sorry."

"I don't remember her," Beau said softly. "Pop saved some pictures for me, but it's not the same."

"I imagine it isn't," Flynn said, feeling like a jerk. *Maybe you should stop talking*, he told himself.

"So," Beau said, after the silence had grown heavy. "Do you want a suggestion? And maybe a helping hand?" He didn't sound angry over Flynn's questions.

Flynn looked from Beau's wrists to his face. Those whiskey eyes weren't any less intense than they had been just a little while ago. "What kind of help?" He had no idea what Beau could possibly offer him, except maybe a sympathetic ear for his drama. *And he's already done that,* Flynn thought.

"If the way you're looking at me is any indication, you seem like you had no idea that you might be the kind of man who leans the other direction," Beau said softly. "So to speak."

Flynn stared at him. "I've never really thought about it." He wouldn't disrespect a guy who had been nothing but kind to him by acting like he didn't know what Beau was talking about. *And it's not like I can afford to make him angry. We're stuck in this cabin together.* He glanced away. The sleet hadn't let up. He'd be amazed if there weren't trees down by morning.

Beau sat up. "I'm not against being your gay experiment."

Flynn's gaze flew back to Beau as his mouth went bone dry. "I'm not into pity fucks," he lied. He so totally *did* want a pity fuck after this stupid day. His *cock* wanted a pity fuck. His hands twitched. It took everything he had in him to keep reclining on the sofa like Beau's suggestion was no big deal.

"Oh, Flynn. It wouldn't be a pity fuck for me," Beau said, voice going low and soft. "You're a fine-looking man." He reached out and put a finger on Flynn's arm, then slid it down until he reached his fingertips.

Flynn's heart banged against his ribs. How could such an innocuous touch feel so damned hot? He licked his lips as he shifted uncomfortably. He wanted that finger on his erection so badly he couldn't keep still. "I don't know what to say." He glanced away. "I don't want you to get hurt."

Beau laughed. "Me? I know exactly what I'm doing."

"I'm on the rebound. That's what this is," Flynn said quickly. He could barely recall what Darlene looked like. And he had no memory of what she tasted like, but he bet Beau tasted like sin. *And regret.*

"I don't care. I like you." Beau leaned closer. The

intensity of his gaze pinned Flynn to the sofa. He couldn't move even if he tried. "You a good man, Flynn, but you're all mixed up. I can help clear some shit up for you."

Flynn held perfectly still as Beau moved his finger down his hip to his leg, but when the man put his palm flat on his thigh, he couldn't stop the moan. "Shit. What are you doing to me?"

"I'm not doing a damned thing." Beau sat back up and lifted his hand away. "Yet." He pulled the blanket off of Flynn. "You need to tell me yes, or this all stops here."

Flynn shuddered. He couldn't think straight anymore. *Am I really contemplating this?* As if from a long way off, he heard himself speak. "Yes."

Beau grinned. "Thank fuck." He stood up and stripped off his shirt. Tiny silver barbells winked out at Flynn from his nipples. His erection poked out his sweatpants.

"Holy shit, you're pierced," Flynn said, staring. The man looked liked a damned cover model. His gaze dropped to Beau's cock. Even from here, and even with the dim lighting, he could tell the guy was well endowed. He thought of anal sex and couldn't hide his wince as he struggled up to a seated position. There was no way he was up for having that thing anywhere near his butthole. No way, no how.

"Don't you worry. We're not going straight for the full monty," Beau said, clearly amused. He dropped to his knees.

"How do you know what I'm thinking?" Flynn asked him. His voice cracked.

"You're thinking the same thing every guy who first sets eyes on me thinks." Beau reached out and pulled Flynn down. "Don't stress. I know what I'm doing."

Flynn couldn't look away from those eyes. "I hope so."

Instead of responding, Beau kissed him. At the first touch of his lips, Flynn gasped. Beau licked inside, and Flynn realized that he'd never, ever really been kissed before. Oh sure, he'd kissed Darlene, and a couple other girlfriends, but he'd never experienced this … this volcano of arousal. He groaned and slid his hands up to cup Beau's head. The small dreadlocks under his palms were soft and springy. Beau smiled against his mouth and kissed him again, not holding back.

"Oh, fuck me," Flynn breathed, when Beau finally let him up for air. He gripped the larger man's biceps, digging his fingers into muscle. Beau wasn't like any woman he'd ever touched. He was hard and impossibly overwhelming.

"No, I'm not going to fuck you," Beau said, biting down Flynn's jaw. "You're going to fuck me."

At those words, Flynn tried to inhale and ended up wheezing. "Jesus, Beau. You sure don't hold back, do you?"

"What would be the point of that?" Beau climbed up and over Flynn, settling his thighs on either side of his hips. "Don't be afraid."

How does he know what I'm feeling? Flynn wondered, but then Beau kissed him again and all rational thought fled. Beau kissed the way some people jumped off cliffs: all in, drunk on adrenaline. *Or maybe that's just me. Maybe that's just what it feels like to kiss this man. To kiss Beau,* Flynn mused, hips jerking. His erection met Beau's considerable weight, and he couldn't resist screwing his body up harder. "God, what is this?"

"This, my friend, is harmony," Beau murmured, moving down until his lips were at Flynn's hip. He knelt up, pulling Flynn's shirt off with one, smooth motion. "Mmm, nice."

"I thought you said 'nice' wasn't a good reason to fuck." Flynn pushed the words out as if he were trying to speak underwater. That's how he felt: completely subsumed by this man. His limbs were heavy. His skin tingled. Every inch of his body cried out for Beau's touch.

Beau put his palms flat on Flynn's chest. "Nice is the way your skin looks under my fingers. Nice is the way you smell." He leaned down and bit one of Flynn's nipples.

Flynn cried out, arching his back.

Beau smirked. "But it isn't the word I'd use to describe what I feel is happening between us." He slid his thumbs under Flynn's sweats. "Lift up."

Flynn obeyed. What else could he do? His body needed this almost more than he needed air. "God, Beau," he murmured when the larger man stripped him of his sweatpants and boxers all at once. His erection sprang out, desperate for attention.

Beau didn't tease him. "Hang onto something."

"What—" Flynn tried to say, but then Beau put his mouth on the tip of his cock and his question fled. The man's mouth was hot and wet and fucking perfect. "Jesus, don't stop," Flynn begged as his scalp prickled.

"I ain't stopping," Beau murmured, hands rolling Flynn's balls. He reached down, fingering at his hole, and Flynn jerked away. Beau got the hint and circled his cock with his fingers instead. He licked a strip up the underside of Flynn's erection. "You taste like desperation." His eyes twinkled as he looked up the length of Flynn's body.

Flynn choked on absolutely nothing as Beau's ridiculous mouth sucked him in again. "You probably do, too," he gasped, wondering what it would be like to suck cock. *You'll likely find out soon enough.*

Beau climbed off of him. "Probably." He looked around. "Ah." He grabbed his duffel and dragged it over.

"What are you doing?" Flynn asked, hands gripping the sofa cushions. If he let go, he didn't know what he'd do. Fall? Tackle Beau? Best not to find out.

"This." Beau held up a condom. "Hang tight." He ripped the foil packet open.

Flynn didn't know how much tighter he could hang on, but he gave it a go, especially when Beau unrolled the condom over his cock. "Oh, Christ," he muttered, closing his eyes against the pleasure. If Beau wasn't careful, he'd come right then and there. "Close," he forced out.

"No, you're not," Beau said, reaching for the duffel again.

Flynn frowned. "Trust me, I am."

Beau lifted his eyebrows as he uncapped a small tube. "Think about Darlene."

Flynn froze. *What the hell?* The image of her face as she stared at him down the long aisle right before she fled their wedding flashed through his mind and his erection wilted slightly. He blinked, and shook his head, glaring at Beau, who had somehow lost his pants. His thick shaft stood out from his body like everything Flynn never knew he wanted. His ex's image disappeared in the face of such blatant masculinity. "That was cruel."

Beau had his fingers in between his legs. "No, it wasn't." He tilted his head. "And that's how you know that it's a good thing you didn't marry her." He nodded towards Flynn's sagging erection.

Flynn sucked in a harsh breath. Beau looked like a damned warrior. Darlene had been a delicate fairy. There was really no comparison. *And what does it mean that I prefer the warrior?* he asked himself, feeling more conflicted than he could ever remember. He wasn't usually so confused, but this situation was beyond anything he'd ever experienced. He'd had no idea he was into guys. *Or maybe I'm just into Beau. Maybe it's the person, not the gender,* he rationalized.

Beau climbed back on top of him, then grasped Flynn's erection firmly. The moment his fingers wrapped around him, Flynn's cock hardened right back up.

"Deep breath."

"What?" Flynn asked, but then he gasped as Beau slowly lowered himself down. The head of his cock touched hot flesh, and then the next thing he knew, the tightest, hottest hole he could never have anticipated surrounded him. "Oh fucking God," he croaked, hands tightening on the cushions. His knuckles cracked, and he bit down on his lip. Hard.

"Oh, yeah. That's fucking perfect," Beau breathed, slowly lowering himself.

Flynn watched Beau's face. The tight frown he'd started off with eased as his body took in more of Flynn's cock. Flynn started panting as his body informed him that it liked this *very fucking much*, and his hips twitched, completely beyond his control. "I'm sorry, I'm sorry," he gasped when Beau looked at him.

"No need," he said in that deep, soft voice of his, and then he hit bottom.

Flynn groaned and clenched his teeth. "Jesus."

"Come on, Flynn," Beau said, leaning down. "You know how to do this."

Flynn let go of the couch, and his hands automatically sought Beau's hips. "Are you sure?" he gritted out. He wanted to fuck and fuck until he lost his goddamn mind. "I don't want to hurt you."

Beau laughed, and the motion set off a burst of

fire in Flynn's groin. "Babe, I ain't no delicate flower."
He leaned down and bit Flynn's shoulder.

Flynn lost it. His hips moved, and he sucked in a
harsh breath as he fucked up inside Beau as hard as he
possibly could. Beau grunted, and Flynn thrust again, and
then again. "Oh fuck," he panted, fingers gripping Beau
too hard. He forced himself to let go, so he could touch
something else, Beau's chest maybe, but then he found
himself gripping the man's wrists, and yanking him
down. "I can't—"

"You can," Beau said, voice low and rough. "You
can, Flynn. You can have this. You can have *me*."

Flynn fucked harder, all his muscles straining.
Beau rode him like a man used to riding nothing tame.
He turned his hands around and weaved their fingers
together. Flynn stared up at him—this man, who'd
flipped his entire worldview upside down—and suddenly
he was coming. He couldn't hold back even if he wanted
to. Pleasure rushed through him in a wave so intense
sparks flittered behind his eyelids. Beau groaned, and he
brought Flynn's fist to his cock. Somehow, Flynn
managed to grab it, and stroke Beau even through his
own orgasm. Beau growled and shuddered as spunk
coated their fingers. Flynn moaned as Beau's muscles
squeezed more pleasure out of him, and he fucked up
inside one last time before Beau slid down on top of him,
boneless and sweaty.

Chapter Four

"So," Beau said, stroking a hand down Flynn's back. They'd managed to pry themselves apart and wash up with the last of the lukewarm water. Flynn had thrown another couple logs on the fire. They'd be good for the rest of the night. Outside, the storm was slowly winding down.

Flynn sighed as if he knew what Beau was going to say. "I know."

"Guys don't just change their orientation. This had to be something you carried with you all along," Beau murmured.

"I never thought about it," Flynn said, knowing that three AM really was the best time to talk about this. The quiet hid his worry. The darkness hid his confusion. *No, not confusion. Embarrassment. How did I not know this about myself?* he wondered, feeling like a fool.

"You shouldn't beat yourself up too much, Flynn," Beau said, voice smooth and soothing. "You're still young."

Flynn snorted. "You say that as if you're some ancient guru." He could feel Beau's smile against his neck. "You're only four years older than me."

"I'm not old, but I've been around the block quite a few times. That makes me *feel* old." Beau inhaled deeply, ruffling Flynn's hair. "You smell good."

"So do you," Flynn replied, knowing even as he did that he'd never be able to go back to a woman's sweet perfume. He liked the size of Beau. He liked the way the man's body felt against his. *I like men,* he thought, rolling the idea around in his head. *I like Beau.* "I think I need to figure some things out," he said softly, wondering what his dad would say when he told him what'd happened. Who in their right mind gets jilted at the altar and immediately falls into bed with a guy not even twenty-four hours later?

"Yeah." Beau kissed Flynn's neck. "But you don't have to figure it all out tonight. You've got time."

Flynn shivered. Beau had the most insane lips he'd ever felt on his skin. He turned his head, and they kissed, and the next thing he knew, he had another hard-on. "God. I've never been this randy. What the hell is it with you?"

Beau chuckled. "Maybe you've just finally woken up." He slid his fingers into Flynn's hair, tugging gently. "I love your hair. It's so soft."

Flynn closed his eyes and let himself live in the moment. Beau felt *right.* "I love your piercings," he murmured, sliding his palms down Beau's chest. He paused to play with the silver barbells, and Beau shivered. "And you have the smoothest skin I've ever touched." He kissed down Beau's neck, then rolled them over until he was on top. He wanted to rub himself all over the man. He wanted to mark him and imprint his scent in his head forever. He inched down, licking as he went, until he ended up between Beau's legs. He grasped the larger man's dusky cock, so different from his pink shaft, suddenly nervous. Beau's erection felt weirdly familiar, and completely strange all at the same time. "I don't know what the fuck I'm doing, here." The words felt like a metaphor for his entire *life,* but he pushed the thought down. He didn't want to think at all right now.

"Do whatever you want," Beau said, breathless.

I did that to him. I made him feel this, Flynn thought, and then he bent down and tasted another man's erection for the first time. Beau smelled musky and sweet, and he tasted like skin and heat. Flynn licked experimentally, and then slid Beau's cock into his mouth and sucked. His own dick ached, and he moaned around the shaft in his mouth.

"Oh yeah, that's it. Suck me." Beau still had his hands in Flynn's hair, but he didn't try to steer. "God, Flynn. You have the most amazing mouth."

Flynn felt Beau's thighs flexing beneath him, and it excited him more than he expected. *I'm aroused by the feeling of another man's cock in my mouth,* he thought, deeply astonished. He sucked some more, trying to take more of Beau into his mouth, but then he went too far and choked. Beau pulled him off, dragging him up until their cocks lined up together. "I wasn't finished," Flynn said, licking his lips.

"Yeah, but I almost finished too soon," Beau said, taking both of their erections in his hands. "Come on. Like this. Fuck into my grip."

Flynn rested his head on Beau's shoulder and let his body figure out what to do. "God," he sighed, as their shafts slid along each other. It wasn't quite enough stimulation to get him off, but that very lack kept him from reaching the edge too quickly. "I love this," he stuttered when Beau twisted his grip. "I love the way you feel."

"Yeah. So do I." Beau moved his hands faster, and Flynn let the larger man show him how to move.

"How did I not know?" Flynn asked, not really expecting an answer, but Beau sighed, even as he stroked faster.

"Some things are too frightening to believe right away," he murmured, kissing Flynn again. "Shh. Let it go, babe."

Flynn closed his eyes. Beau's hands moved faster, and faster again. Soon enough Flynn was close. "I'm there, Beau. I'm right fucking there," he said, digging his fingers into Beau's shoulders.

"I know. I've got you. Let it go." Beau turned his

head and kissed him, and Flynn's orgasm rushed through him, long and slow and sweet. He felt like he was flying, or maybe surfing, and Beau was the wave. He let the pleasure take him, and Beau kept him right on the crest of it for far longer than he thought possible.

****

When Flynn woke up the next morning, the first thing he realized was that he was cold. The next thing he realized was that it wasn't morning, it was mid-afternoon. The third thing was that he was alone, and that wasn't right, not after the night he'd just had. He stared up at the ceiling, vaguely confused, then glanced at the fireplace. The fire had gone out.

"Beau?" he called, but no one answered. He sat up, and the blanket fell to his waist. He grimaced. They hadn't got up after the last time they'd made love, and dried jizz itched down his abdomen. "Beau? You there?" He stood up and padded naked to the kitchen.

Storm's gone, he thought squinting. The cabin seemed strangely huge, even with the sunlight streaming in through the windows. When he saw the paper tacked to the refrigerator, he frowned. He reached out, not recognizing the handwriting.

But then, I wouldn't, would I? We barely know each other, he thought, even as his heart protested. Somehow, he'd managed to lose a fiancée and fall in love with someone completely unexpected all in the course of one impossible day. He stared at the paper. *Flynn,*

Forgive me. I had to go. I woke up early and realized that I was being a selfish bastard. I like you. I want to stay with you. Sometimes you meet someone and the most unexpected connection arises out of nowhere, and that's how I feel about you. I wanted to stay, but I worried that I would fall in love with you so hard and so fast that you would not have the time and space to figure out what you truly want. I woke up early and realized that I wanted to stay with you forever. So when I saw that the storm had ended, I called a ride. I'm heading back to LA, but I'll be in touch.

Love, Beau

What the fuck, Flynn thought, staring at the word *love* as if it would leap off the page and bite him if he looked away. "Shit," he muttered, about to crumple the paper, but then he turned it over and froze. Beau had done a pencil drawing of him sleeping, and though the man hadn't shied away from showing every last detail of his nude body, the thing that really hit him was the expression on his face. Flynn flushed. He didn't know he could look like that. He looked like a stranger—someone more interesting than he knew he actually was, like a man who'd been through some shit. He looked like someone's lover. He traced a finger over the line of his arm. His hand shook. He wasn't that person, was he? He listened to his heart pound for a long time.

"Beau, you idiot," he said finally, swallowing hard. "How the hell are you going to keep in touch? I never gave you my fucking number." He set the paper down on the counter, very, very gently. It took a long time for him to figure out why he felt like he couldn't breathe.

****

One month later, Flynn's father set down the length of pipe he was using as leverage for a particularly stubborn bolt and sighed. He pulled off the socket and set the wrench on the floor. The car on the lift was an old Porsche, and it needed a new exhaust system. In order to get to it, they had to take off the wheels first.

"What? I thought you got it started?" Flynn said, holding a can of lube ready. He'd told his father a thousand times that it was easier to spray and let the stuff penetrate before hammering at the damned bolts, but his dad was a stubborn man. "Maybe you should've used the impact wrench."

"The impact wrench would've broken the bolt." His father shook his head, looking at Flynn as though he had a lot more to say.

But I'm in no mood to talk, Flynn thought, ducking his father's gaze. He hadn't been in the mood to talk in weeks. His thoughts skittered to the memory of that night in the cabin, but he pushed the images down with the ease of several weeks' practice, which basically meant: not at all well. Beau haunted him, the fucker.

Flynn's father sighed and stretched, twisting his lower back, then he wiped his hands on a rag. "All right, I'm tired of waiting. Spill it, Flynn." The older man's eyes were more hazel than his, but otherwise, Flynn knew that he was looking at his future self in twenty-five years or so. Give or take.

He frowned. "What are you talking about? You want the lube or not?" He held out the can. He knew his father wouldn't take it.

His dad looked at him steadily. "Darlene picked up the last of her stuff from your place?"

What? That's what he wants to know? Flynn put the can of lube on the workbench. "Yeah. I know I told you. She came for the last few boxes on the weekend." Flynn didn't understand why his father was asking him again. "All her stuff is gone." He cocked his head. "Did Mom put you up to this? I know she was really upset about the wedding." Guilt twisted in his gut. To be honest, that's the part that really disturbed him the most about Darlene's last-minute exit from their relationship. He'd hated disappointing his mother.

His father shook his head. "You don't seem all

that bothered."

"Why would I be bothered? I'm glad she got the last of her stuff out of my house." He didn't add *good riddance* because he figured it was implied.

His father exhaled and walked over to the rack of tools along the back wall of the shop. "Flynn, you've been moping around for the past few weeks."

Flynn rolled his eyes. "My fiancée ran away from me at the altar, right before we got married. Of course I'm feeling crappy."

His dad gave him a look that told Flynn he wasn't buying it. "If her leaving bothered you that much, you wouldn't be so cool about her picking up her stuff." He leaned back against the rack. "What happened when you were at the cabin?"

Flynn's face burned. He still couldn't think about Beau without losing his composure. Just the barest hint of the memory of that night made his cock perk up, and that was the last thing he needed with his father grilling him. "I don't know what you mean. I went up there and had a quiet few days. End of story."

His dad shook his head. "Flynn."

Shit. He's not buying it. Flynn started pacing. "What do you want me to say?"

"I want you to talk, because you look like you need it," his father said, not backing down.

Flynn stopped and eyed his dad. His father had no idea what he was asking for. "Look, Dad, I appreciate it, but I'm going through some things." He scrubbed a hand through his hair. "I don't know if you even want to hear about it."

"Flynn, you're my son. Of course I want to listen to you." His father walked over to the mini fridge and stuck a hand inside. He came out with two beers. "Here. Sit down. Have a drink."

Flynn sighed, but he wouldn't refuse beer. "It's the middle of the day."

"So? We own the place." His father looked around pointedly.

True story. Flynn sat down on the beat-up sofa they kept in the back corner of the shop and cracked open the can. He took a long sip, then set the beer on the floor. "I don't know how to start."

His father swallowed his mouthful of beer. "This isn't about Darlene."

Flynn sighed. "No." He rubbed his face. "She did the right thing, you know. Taking off. We never should have dated, let alone planned to get married." He tipped his head back. "Thank God it was a really small wedding. And we never had a wedding shower, so no gifts to return. I wonder what Darlene's parents did with all the food? I really appreciate you picking up my stuff from their house for me. I guess they cancelled the reception."

"You're deflecting." His father leaned back against the cracked vinyl. "What happened at the cabin, Flynn?"

Flynn kept talking. Maybe he could distract his father with useless information. "There was that storm, you know? I drove up from Boston, and then it started sleeting. When I got there, they'd already winterized the other cabins because none of the other guests for that last week had made it through the weather." He took another sip of beer. He needed the fortification. "Except this one guy whose reservation they'd screwed up. He was booked for next year." Flynn shook his head. "I don't know whose fault it was, but the guy had nowhere to go."

"Now we're getting somewhere," Flynn's father muttered under his breath.

Flynn glared at him.

His father didn't even have the grace to look sorry. "So, he stayed with you," he said, as if he'd expected nothing less. Of course he'd hone right in on the heart of the matter.

"Yup." Flynn closed his eyes and tipped his head back. "He's an artist. And a photographer."

After a long moment of silence, his father prodded him. "And?"

Flynn looked at his dad. "And what?"

"And something happened, right?"

He knows. Flynn's face heated. "Sort of."

His dad laughed. "Flynn, I wasn't born yesterday."

I can't do this, Flynn thought, pushing to his feet. *I can't talk to my dad about this.* The memory of Beau's soft lips on his burned through his mind.

"Did you at least get the guy's number?" his dad asked him.

Flynn spun around. His father looked amused. "Are you laughing at me?"

"I've been wondering how long it would take you to figure it out," his father said, eyes twinkling. "In all seriousness, I knew you were into guys when you were in high school. So did your mother." All the humor left his face. "I really worried about you with Darlene."

Flynn stared at his father. "You knew? Mom knew? How?" He squeezed his head. "*I* didn't even know. What the fuck?"

His father shook his head. "I don't know. I just had a feeling. You never seemed to really have a spark with any of those girls you dated."

Spark. There's that word again, Flynn thought. "I don't know what to say."

"I'm not the person you should be trying to talk to," his father pointed out. "Did you get his number?"

Flynn grimaced. "No. He left before we could really talk about things." He started pacing again. "He said he'd be in touch, but he doesn't have my contact information. We exchanged names, but nothing else." He sighed. "Maybe I'm just rebounding from Darlene."

"You can't rebound from someone you were never in love with. Why don't you look this guy up? There's this thing called the Internet, you know. It's not like you have to hire a private investigator to hunt him down," his father said, and then he grinned. "And if he knows your name, he can look up the shop. You're the one who set up our website, in case you don't remember."

Flynn rolled his eyes at his father. "Very funny. I'm not as old as you. My memory works just fine." He paused for a moment, then forged ahead. "How are you okay with this?" Flynn felt as if his entire worldview had just shifted on its axis. "You're not upset. Aren't most parents upset when they find out their kids bats for the other team?" He was deflecting again because this had to be the most awkward conversation he'd ever had with his father. He knew his dad wouldn't mind him being gay, but maybe if he could get the old man to defend himself, he would stop asking uncomfortable questions.

"Flynn, look," his father said, standing up. "I grew up in the 70s and 80s. I'm not some asshole who doesn't know that sometimes love happens in unexpected places."

"But what about Mom?" Flynn had to ask. The look on her face when Darlene took off haunted him.

"What about her?"

Flynn scowled at his father, and the older man sighed. "She's totally fine with it. The only thing she worries about is you getting hurt."

"You're sure about that?" Flynn started pacing

again. He couldn't keep still. He was all torn up inside over a guy he'd known maybe twenty-four hours, tops. "Shit."

"I'm positive that your mother wants you to be happy." His father gathered up their cans and tossed them into the dingy recycle bin near the fridge. "Look this guy up. You say he's an artist? I'm sure he has some sort of online portfolio."

Beau did. Flynn had already looked him up, but he was too chickenshit to reach out. What if he remembered that night all wrong? What if it had been just a hookup for Beau? *Don't be stupid. He fucking drew you a love note,* his inner voice reminded him.

"Yeah," Flynn said, rubbing his face again. And now he probably had grease all over himself. "Dammit. I don't know what happened. We talked a lot. I told him about Darlene. And Beau was just…" He trailed off, remembering. "Perfect. I've never met anyone like him."

"Sounds like when I met your mother," his father said, voice soft. "Call him. You only live once, Flynn." His father walked back to the partly dismantled car and crouched down to retrieve the wrench.

"Call him?" Flynn stared at his dad. "That's it?"

"It's not that complicated." His father smiled up at him. "What more do you want? Written directions?"

Flynn's face heated. "I, uh, sort of have that, too." He smiled wryly. "He wrote me a note. And drew a picture of me."

His dad laughed. "Jesus, Flynn. The guy practically gave you a map. Stop pussyfooting around the situation and call him. What could it hurt? He either says yes or no, and either way, you'll have an answer and hopefully stop moping around the place like somebody pissed in your cereal."

Way to make a point, Dad, Flynn thought, but he

nodded. "Yeah." He grabbed the pipe and handed it to his dad. "Okay. I'll call him." *Like that's so easy.* "He lives in LA. Even if he's interested, it's going to be complicated."

"You realize the reason this is so hard for you is because this is the first time you've ever had any skin in the game, Flynn," his dad said, yanking on the wrench. "With all those girls, you never really felt anything. All that's changed now, with this Beau guy."

True. Flynn swallowed the lump in his throat. "Can we please stop talking about my emotions? I may be gay now, but I'm still a dude."

His father laughed. "Yeah, I'm not having fun either." He gave the wrench another yank, and the bolt turned. "That's it. There she goes." He glanced at his son. "Or for you, there *he* goes."

Flynn rolled his eyes. "You're lame."

"If I am, so are you," his dad retorted.

"Flynn? There's a guy out here looking for you," Anna, their part time receptionist, interrupted them before Flynn could escalate their banter. She stood in the doorway between the shop and the front office.

"Does he have an appointment?" Flynn asked, confused. He thought the entire day was clear. Usually their clients called ahead. It was rare for them to just show up. "What kind of car?"

Anna shook her head. "No kind. He said he's not here about a car. He just wants to talk to you."

"What?" Flynn didn't understand. "Who is it?"

Anna opened the door wider, and Flynn's heart abruptly tried to leap out of his chest.

"I can't believe you don't remember my name, Flynn," Beau said, smiling.

Chapter Five

Flynn stared. There wasn't enough air in the shop. Why wasn't there enough air? He needed it in order to think. "Beau?" he croaked as his heart climbed up into his throat.

"You *do* remember," Beau said, voice low and smooth. He smiled, and then his gaze shifted to Flynn's father. "You must be his dad." He laughed. "You guys could be twins."

Flynn's father smiled. "Twins separated by twenty-five years, maybe." He looked at his son and smirked. "And I like to think that I'm a little smarter than my son." He walked forward, hand outstretched. "You must be Beau, the guy Flynn is all torn up about. I'm Jack."

Beau shook his hand. "Pleased to meet you, Mr. Russell."

"Call me Jack. I have a feeling we're going to be seeing a lot of each other." He looked at Flynn, eyes twinkling.

Flynn flushed. "Dad, this is Beau Green."

"The artist." His father nodded as Flynn wondered when his life had become a damned romance novel. Could this be any stranger? Beau looked like a cool drink of water: tall, dark, and handsome. He wore a silvery blue shirt and black jeans, and he had his duffel with him. His leather jacket, far too thin for the winter weather, hung open. His eyes gleamed behind the thin silver frames of his ridiculous glasses. Flynn wanted to climb him. He wanted to dismantle Beau's composure until he looked as disheveled on the outside as Flynn felt on the inside.

"Flynn, I think you're done here for the day. I've got this bolt out, and I can handle the rest of the exhaust myself," his father said, heading back to the car on the lift.

Flynn swallowed, forcing his brain to work. "Thanks, Dad," he said, embarrassed and hopeful and confused. *Do I kiss him? Shake his hand?* He stopped right in front of Beau, afraid that maybe the guy was an illusion.

"I'm real," Beau said, so softly Flynn could barely hear him.

He reached out, and Beau grasped his hand, pulling him in. Flynn let him, falling into an embrace that was equal parts desperation and relief. "God, Beau. What are you doing here?"

Beau let him go. "I couldn't stay away any longer." He shook his head, eyes going dark and worried. "I hope I gave you enough time. I really tried to give you space."

"Space?" Flynn stared at him. "I've never felt so fucking depressed in my life as I have the past four weeks. I don't need space."

Beau frowned, trying to step back, but Flynn wouldn't let him go. "You're sad about Darlene?" His face closed down.

"Who's Darlene?" Flynn snorted, holding onto Beau's arms. "No, you idiot." He gave the larger man a little shake. "I missed *you*. Jesus."

Beau's expression went from tight to hopeful. "You better not be fucking with me, Flynn."

Flynn shook his head. "No joke." He glanced back as his father. His old man was humming to himself as he picked up the impact wrench. "I literally just told my dad about you, like, five minutes ago." He winced when his father started in on the rest of the bolts. The impact wrench was not a quiet tool. "Come on. We can't talk here." He knew his dad had started making a racket on purpose, and it worked.

"Who said anything about talking?" Beau retorted, but he let Flynn pull him out of the doorway and through the office.

"I'm taking off, Anna. Dad's still in the back," Flynn told the receptionist, not slowing.

She smiled at him. "Good. You deserve some time off."

Flynn waved, then dragged Beau out to his car. He didn't bother with his coat. It didn't matter that it was freezing out—he felt like he was burning up. "How did you even get here?" he asked Beau, not seeing any new vehicles in the shop's lot.

"Uber from the airport," Beau replied, tossing his duffel in the back as soon as Flynn unlocked the vehicle. Flynn watched him smile up at the trees that lined the street. They'd finally dropped the last of their leaves. The sky was cloudy and threatening cold rain. "I forgot how much I liked Pittsburgh," Beau said glancing around. "Beautiful city."

"Oakland is definitely one of the nicer parts of the city," Flynn agreed, though it wasn't a nice day. The tail end of November was never nice in this part of the country. The weather was cold and damp and grey, but for the first time in weeks, he felt light. His feet carried him over to Beau, and he crowded the man up against the passenger's side door. "Fuck, Beau," he murmured, then dragged his head down for a kiss. He didn't care if anyone saw them. He didn't care about anything except Beau being right here, right now, at the most unexpected moment. "I can't believe you're actually here."

Beau kissed him back, then nibbled on Flynn's lower lip. "Like I said, I couldn't stay away any longer. I'm a patient man, but I'm not *that* patient."

Flynn forced himself to let Beau go. "I'm taking

you home."

"Okay," Beau said agreeably as he opened the car door.

Flynn wondered how far he could take this. "And you're moving in with me. Screw LA. You belong here."

"No problem." Beau slid into the passenger's seat and buckled up. "Where's home?"

"Beeler Street," Flynn said as he got in and started the car. "Near CMU. You should know the neighborhood."

"I do. Nice place. Quiet." Beau started whistling. "You know, my father moved near Zelienople when he remarried. It'll be nice to be around as my little brothers grow up."

"Yeah? Sounds like you have it all planned out," Flynn couldn't resist saying.

"I do." Beau put a hand on Flynn's thigh.

Flynn swerved, almost hitting the curb, and then a parked car, and he cursed under his breath as his cock went from interested to desperate. He couldn't stop grinning. "And we're probably going to get married. You know that, right? I need to cheer up my mom. She was really bummed when my ex ran away. Also, watch the hand, you're very distracting."

"Marriage works for me. My brothers will love being ring bearers," Beau said, half-laughing.

Flynn smiled so wide his face hurt. *I know I'm moving fast, but this is Beau. And it feels right.*

"And by the way, I've been distracted and miserable for a month," Beau continued, not moving his hand. "I couldn't sleep. The air in LA was too hot. It was too sunny. Everything felt wrong."

Flynn nodded. "I know. I don't know why you live there." He laughed, amazed that Beau didn't deck him for being a total shit. "LA sucks."

"I don't live there anymore," Beau said, grinning. "And I can work from anywhere." He looked out the window. It had started raining. "I love this city."

"I love you," Flynn said, then clamped his mouth shut. He glanced over, heart in his throat, only to find Beau looking at him as if he'd just handed the guy the moon.

"That works for me," Beau said, voice going soft. He licked his lips. "Because when I went back to LA, I felt like I left my heart with you in that cabin."

Flynn swallowed hard, then forced himself to drive instead of answering. The minute it took for him to turn down the street where he lived felt like an eternity. "Well. You're home now," he said softly. He pulled into his driveway and turned off the car.

"Am I?" Beau asked.

Flynn nodded. "Yeah." His voice broke. "I don't know why you'd want to live anywhere else."

"I don't want to live anywhere else." Beau reached out, and suddenly they were kissing.

For the first time in a month, Flynn didn't feel hollow. "Let's go inside," he gasped, tearing his mouth away. The gearshift had pressed a bruise into his hip. Two grown men couldn't make out in the front seat of a car and not come away injured, but it was so damned hard to let go of Beau. He un-fisted his fingers and released Beau's jacket. "Now." He stepped out of the car.

"Agreed," Beau said, opening his door. He grabbed his duffel and followed Flynn up the front walk.

Flynn unlocked the front door, and Beau shoved him inside. He dropped his bag and slammed Flynn up against the wall. "Nice house," he said, not even looking around. He kissed Flynn again, ravaging his lips. "It's got a roof."

"You like the roof?" Flynn asked, laughing.

"Yes, I do. It's raining. Making love in November can be very inconvenient without a roof," Beau replied.

Flynn grinned as he sank his fingers into Beau's biceps. "Okay, yeah. Whatever. It's a house. It doesn't leak." He kicked the front door shut and dragged Beau upstairs. "Your new bedroom," he said, opening the door to his room. He dragged Beau over to his double bed and pushed him down onto it, then climbed on top of him.

"We're buying a new bed," Beau said, groaning when Flynn's groin met his. "A king sized."

"Tomorrow," Flynn said, shoving at Beau's coat. "Off."

Beau laughed and took off his coat. "Impatient much?"

"Shut up." Flynn was already working on Beau's pants.

Beau gasped when his cock sprang out and Flynn fisted it. "God, Flynn. You'd better be damned sure about this."

Flynn gritted his teeth. "I am." He was never letting Beau go again. "If you don't give me your number I will hunt you down and make you sorry."

"I drew you a picture. That's better than a cell phone number." Beau reached up and grabbed the neck of Flynn's shop t-shirt. "I'm going to rip this off you if you don't get naked right now."

He would, Flynn realized, taking in the almost feral gleam in Beau's gaze. He stood up and stripped in five seconds flat, then dragged Beau's pants off. "I can't wait," he said, thrusting the moment his cock met Beau's.

"Me neither," Beau said, hands going to Flynn's ass. "Oh God, I'm right there."

Flynn moved faster, reveling in the feel of Beau's skin touching every inch of his body. "I'm sorry," he gasped as his balls drew up against his body. He couldn't hold on any longer. He groaned as pleasure tore out of him. He felt as though his heart was too full for his chest.

Beau growled, grinding up into him as he came. Warm wetness spread between them. It took a while to catch their breaths.

"What are you sorry for?" Beau asked after a while, sighing as Flynn slid off him.

He didn't go far. He slung a leg and arm over the larger man, because he still needed convincing that Beau wasn't just a dream. *He's not going anywhere,* he tried to tell himself, but a tiny niggle of worry still pricked at him. "I should've looked for you." He held onto Beau's forearm as though he would fall out of the bed if he let go. "I shouldn't have spent an entire month wandering around, confused and miserable."

"You needed the time to figure yourself out," Beau said softly. "I knew that, even if you didn't."

Flynn shrugged. "I don't know." He rolled onto his back, dragging Beau's arm with him. "I'm twenty-six. I should know what I want by now." He smiled wryly. "But I guess life isn't always that easy."

Beau snorted. "No. Easy is for fools and people who think they know it all." He rolled closer and kissed Flynn's jaw. "I'm here now. You had enough time to miss me, and I'm not going anywhere."

Flynn smiled, feeling his doubts fading the more Beau spoke. "Did you tell your dad about me?"

Beau laughed. "Hell, yeah. I started wrapping up my last few contracts in LA the moment I got back. I've already got feelers out in New York and Philadelphia, as well as Pittsburgh."

Flynn's eyebrows rose. "You were that sure of me?" He couldn't even imagine someone wanting him that bad.

"I was sure of myself," Beau said, smiling. "I wasn't about to give up on you."

Flynn couldn't help it. He let his grin spread across his face. "Huh."

"What about you? Is your dad okay with me?" Beau asked. "With us? He seemed pretty chill earlier."

Flynn shook his head, still bemused. "Yeah. He said that he and Mom knew I was gay since I was in high school. You could've knocked me over with a toothpick." He laughed. "He said he was really worried when I got together with Darlene, and now that I think back on it, I remember him dropping hints the whole time I was with her. I'm such an idiot."

"You're not an idiot. You figured it out," Beau said, drawling a little. "Eventually." He waited a beat. "With help. With a *lot* of help."

"Hey!" Flynn went up on his elbow. "If you're going to live here, you have to be nice to me."

Beau plastered a shit eating grin on his face as he sat up. "Babe, don't worry. I'm going to be very, *very* nice to you. As often as possible." With those words, he pulled Flynn back down onto the bed and kissed him in the best possible way.

Flynn shivered. *Sparks,* he thought, licking into Beau's mouth. His lover groaned, and then Flynn couldn't think at all anymore, but it was okay. He didn't have to.

The End

THE DRIVE

Close Proximity, 3

Erin. M. Leaf

Copyright © 2018

Chapter One

"So, Dad, remember that internship I told you about?" Portia's excitement came through loud and clear, despite the crappy cell phone connection. "The one I got waitlisted for?"

Liam Humphrey glanced at his phone as he drove, already knowing that the plans he'd made with his daughter and her friend were toast. Her picture smiled up at him from his phone's display: blonde and brown-eyed in direct contrast to his dark hair and grey eyes. The question was, did he pull off the next exit and turn around now? Or keep driving? *Either way, my week is about to suck.* He sighed quietly, equal parts proud of his daughter and disappointed for himself.

"Let me guess, they called you?" he asked, faking enthusiasm. He was happy for her, he really was, but he'd also been looking forward to spending time with her. She had one more year of college, and then who knew where she'd go?

"Yes!" she said excitedly. "I'm already packed up. I'm shipping all my stuff home to Mom's place, so you won't have to worry about anything."

Liam sighed again. Where did his daughter get the idea that he found her *or* her belongings tiresome? Now he'd have to negotiate with his ex to get his daughter's clothes back from her greedy, idiotic grasp. Not for the first time, he cursed his stupid dick for ever getting distracted by Charlotte's pretty face. Of course, he'd been all of nineteen at the time and still grieving the sudden horrible end of his first relationship, so he had to cut his younger self a bit of slack. No man was entirely in charge of his libido at that age. "Darling, I'd be happy to deal with your stuff, anytime you want. You know this."

"I know, Dad, but I also know how busy you are. It's not easy running a nightclub." Portia clicked her tongue. "And I know that you're usually asleep in the mornings. Those delivery guys always show up at nine AM where you live."

She had a point. "I can go without sleep for a day or two for my only daughter." Liam kept driving. "I'm still coming by to see you, even if you're not coming home with me. I haven't seen you in months, and I'm already most of the way there."

Portia laughed. "I had a feeling you'd say that. I told my friend Charlie that you'd still give him a ride home."

"Of course, darling." Liam squinted a little against the glare of the desert. He was happy to help out. He'd never met her friend, but Portia had been telling him tales of the guy's dating escapades for the past six months. Seems the guy really had trouble with girls, and his daughter had befriended the man. Portia had a soft heart.

"I knew you'd say that, Daddy," Portia told him, a hint of amusement in her voice.

Liam knew what she was thinking, but he refused to entertain the thought that he was a nice guy. Nightclub owners and businessmen who made as much as he did weren't *nice.* "We'll go to dinner before we head home," he said, already contemplating the delightful fish tacos they served at his favorite restaurant in Flagstaff. It was a quaint little city, and he wasn't disappointed that his daughter had chosen to go to Northern Arizona University. She'd loved the location, and of course, the proximity to Lowell Observatory.

Although how I managed to spawn a child interested in physics and astronomy remains a mystery to me, he thought, bemused, as always, by his daughter's impressive brain. She certainly didn't get it from her mother. Charlotte's goal in life had always been to bang the most attractive man she could find, and she used her considerable assets ruthlessly to achieve that objective. She had brains, but she always turned them towards selfish goals. "So, it's off to Hawaii then, for you?"

"I've already got my plane tickets," Portia told him. "I'm leaving later tonight, so we're not going to be able to do dinner, though. Which sucks. I was wishing for those fish tacos." She sounded disappointed.

Damn. Liam grimaced. "Ah, well. The internship is only for a month, and then we can stuff ourselves full of tacos until we can't move." His phone GPS pinged an alert, and he smoothly transferred lanes in preparation for his exit. "Does Charlie know you're foisting him off on me?"

"I'm not foisting him, Dad. I'm simply helping a friend out," she said, then laughed. "You're too nice, you know. Most fathers wouldn't be so accommodating."

There's that word. He winced. "Yes, well. I'm easily bored, you know. I enjoy meeting new people," he said. It was the truth, after all, and easier to swallow than the idea that he was *nice.*

"I know, and I told him that, but he's a bit shy. He's feeling all guilty and whatnot."

"I'll sort him out," Liam assured her. She'd been talking about Charlie for months—he almost felt like he knew the guy. He glanced at the map on his phone. "I'll be there in five, darling. Make sure he's ready, all right?"

"You'll go easy on the guy, right, Dad?" Portia asked.

"I don't know what you mean." Liam frowned. "I don't eat babies for breakfast, Portia."

She laughed. "Oh, it's not that."

"Well, what are you implying then, my dear?" Liam had no idea what she was getting at.

"You're going to like him."

Well, I should hope so, Liam thought. The guy was his daughter's friend, after all. "Portia, you're not making any sense." He took the next exit, and turned left at the light.

"I think you're going to like him, that's all." His daughter's tone on the word *like* finally clued him in on what she meant.

Liam rolled his eyes. "I'm not going to hook up with your friend, Portia. As if." He continued north on Milton Road until he reached the cemetery, and then took another right. "Not only is that highly inappropriate, I don't have time for dating. You know that. I'm happy with my work and with my lovely daughter." He hoped she'd drop the subject, honestly. He was already in a mood because he wouldn't get to spend any time with her, and this line of conversation wasn't helping. He had no desire to discuss his love life, or lack thereof, with his child, even if she was fully adult now.

"Well, I wish you *would* date, Dad. I worry about you getting lonely," Portia said, her voice going quiet. "I still can't believe Mom left because you're bi. That's just ridiculous."

Liam took a deep breath, then let it out again. He was *not* going to arrive at Portia's apartment all moody and sad. The situation with his ex had been quite a bit more complicated than his daughter knew, but it was true that Charlotte had used his sexuality as an excuse to leave. "It's nothing to do with you, darling. I've told you that a thousand times. We were too young to get married."

"It's still stupid."

It is completely stupid, but that's Charlotte. Liam took the next left and slowed as he neared her apartment building. "I'm nearly there, Portia. Is your friend ready?" He heard rustling, and knew she'd been talking outside on her balcony.

"He's ready, Dad," his daughter replied.

Liam could hear a man talking in the background, and then his daughter laughed again. "No, no, Charlie. He's entirely fine with taking you to Las Vegas. I promise." More murmuring. "No, geez, will you relax? My dad is not scary. You'll like him. I promise."

Liam shook his head, smiling. Portia was the best thing that ever happened to him, even if he'd had to deal with Charlotte to get her. "I'm hanging up now, Portia," he said, just as he pulled into a parking space. Her apartment was on a quiet street, within walking distance of the university.

"Okay, Dad. See you soon," Portia said, sounding distracted, and then the line went dead.

Liam turned off the car, and sat for a moment to

get his emotions under control. He didn't want his daughter thinking he wasn't happy for her. He took a deep breath, and then let it out again, willing his disappointment to dissipate with it. He'd see his daughter in a month or so, and it would be lovely. Right now, she needed her father to support her.

"All right then. Time to do the right thing," he murmured, exiting the car. He whistled as he walked up to the door, smiling when it buzzed as soon as he arrived on the step. "Watching for me, hmm?" he murmured. He entered, then took the stairs two at a time. When he reached the second-floor landing, he turned right and went down the short hall. His daughter's apartment door stood open.

"Portia?" he called as he walked inside. After several hours of driving, it felt good to stretch his legs. "Where are you, darling?"

"Right here, Dad," she said, walking out of her bedroom.

Liam grinned and opened his arms. She ran into them, and he lifted her off the ground as he gave her a big hug. "Oh, my goodness. You grew!" he exclaimed, smiling down at her.

She rolled her eyes and whacked his arm. "I did not. You just have a terrible memory. You think I'm twelve." Her brown eyes twinkled up at him. "You must be getting old if you can't remember things anymore."

He snorted. "Thirty-nine is not old." He gave her another hug, then froze for a moment. A man stood near the door to the balcony, watching them. "Ah. You must be Charlie," Liam said, letting his daughter go.

"Hello." The man nodded, smiling shyly.

Liam stared. The guy had tousled brown hair and brown eyes, and at first glance, he was nothing special, but something about him intrigued Liam. His tight t-shirt and jeans highlighted an extremely fit body, and Liam had the sudden urge to grab the guy in order to see if he felt as solid as he looked. *Ah, hell,* he thought, as his cock twitched, pressing against the placket of his black jeans uncomfortably. *Portia was right.* His immediate attraction to the young man threw him off balance, and he glanced at his daughter, only to find her grinning knowingly at him. He scowled slightly, but her grin only widened.

"Dad, this is Charlie Bright. Charlie, this is my dad, Liam." Portia dragged Liam over to her friend. "Don't worry. I promised you he doesn't bite."

Except I do bite. Sometimes, Liam thought, very privately.

"Nice to meet you," Charlie said, proving that despite his shyness, he wasn't a pushover. He held out his hand.

Liam kicked himself mentally, dragging his mind out of the gutter, and smiled. "I'm delighted to meet you, Charlie. My daughter has been singing your praises for months now." His voice dipped into a lower register without him even trying, and he cleared his throat softly. He could feel his daughter's smug resignation radiating from her in waves, and she got that from *him*, so he really couldn't complain about her attitude, but he wanted to, he really, really did.

"Are you sure you don't have time for dinner, darling?" he asked her instead of calling her out on her smugness, and too, he needed to distract himself from the delightful young man he desperately wanted to put his hands all over. *No, and no. He's your daughter's friend,* he reminded himself sternly. *Hands off.*

"I'm sorry, I can't. I have to finish packing in the next half hour, and then get to the airport," she said apologetically.

Liam sighed, again disappointed, but also unsurprised. "I'll miss you."

Portia's smile slipped a bit. "Oh, Dad. Stop. You're going to make me cry." She slipped into his arms and hugged him tightly.

Liam hugged her back. She didn't feel like his little girl anymore—she was strong and confident, and that's what he wanted, right? "It's only for a month, darling. And you're going to have a fantastic time staring up at the stars," he said, letting her go. That's what parents did, after all.

Portia laughed, eyes bright. "You do realize that most of the staring is done at computer monitors, right?" She patted his arm and headed for her room. "Come talk to me while I finish packing."

Liam smiled wryly at Charlie. "The princess commands, and so we must obey."

Charlie snorted, but they both followed her to her room anyway.

Chapter Two

Liam hummed under his breath with the music as he eased onto the highway. He'd seen his daughter into the airport shuttle, and her excitement over her new internship had finally soothed away most of his disgruntlement. He couldn't hold her back. His job as her father was to give her his support, not his worries. So, he'd sucked it up and wished her the best, and then he'd slipped her a thousand in cash on the sly. He smiled and hummed louder as he imagined her finding it in her bag when she unpacked.

"I really appreciate the ride, Mr. Humphrey," Charlie said, in that soft voice of his.

Liam turned the music's volume down a tad. "Oh, please, no. Not the dreaded Mister title. Call me Liam. I know I'm old, but I'm not ancient," Liam said to his passenger. He glanced over to find Charlie rubbing a finger down the soft leather of the Land Rover's seat. He shivered. Charlie's hands were competent and strong. He shook his head. He had to stop this. He hadn't dated a guy in twenty years, since before he'd married Portia's mother. He might be bisexual, but he'd spent the vast majority of his life either alone or with a woman.

"Liam," Charlie repeated, sending a shiver of lust down Liam's spine. "I really appreciate the ride."

This isn't the ride I would like to give you, Liam mused, rolling his tongue around his mouth. He pushed the thought down. "Where are you staying in Vegas? Portia tells me that you're not from Sin City," he said, trying to distract himself from his unexpected arousal. He hadn't been this randy in ages. *Clearly, I need to get laid.* He squinted as he drove, then grabbed his sunglasses from the visor. The sun was still fairly high in the sky though it was late afternoon, and they were driving west.

"I'm hoping that my aunt and uncle are home," Charlie said, looking out the window.

Hoping? Liam frowned. "You don't know?"

Charlie shrugged. "My parents died when I was fifteen. My aunt and uncle took me in for a few years, but since college, they've been pretty hands off. I've been on my own for a while now."

Liam stared at him a moment before wrenching his gaze back to the road. "Jesus. I'm sorry."

"Thanks. It was a long time ago." Charlie shifted in his seat.

"Not *that* long ago," Liam muttered, still horrified that the guy had lost his parents at such a young age. He couldn't imagine Portia having to fend for herself at fifteen. *He* hadn't lost his parents until a few years ago, and it was still difficult at times.

Charlie looked over at him. "I'm twenty-one. It really was a while ago. I'm okay on my own."

Wow. He's had to grow up fast, Liam mused. "You're two years older than my daughter."

Charlie nodded. "Yeah?"

Liam shook his head. Charlie was entirely adult, but Liam still felt decidedly strange about his attraction to the guy. "Nothing. I'm just surprised."

"Portia and I ... you realize we're not dating," Charlie said, then chuckled. "I asked her out. She turned me down flat. She said, and I quote, 'You're more my dad's type than mine.'"

"What?" Liam laughed, wanting to be surprised, but not. His daughter wasn't shy about speaking her mind. "She said that?"

Charlie nodded. "She did."

"That little shit," Liam said. He had to hand it to her, she had balls. "I haven't dated anyone in a long time. Not since her mother and I divorced ten years ago."

Charlie frowned. "Wait, what? You were married to a woman?"

Liam rolled his eyes. "My darling daughter conveniently forgot to mention that, hmm?"

Charlie scrubbed his face with the palm of his hand. "I'm so confused right now." He took a deep breath. "I thought—" He frowned. "Hell. I don't know *what* I thought."

"I'm not gay," Liam said, just to screw with the guy. Sure enough, Charlie's face pinked up. He was adorable. And hot. Why that combination revved his engine was a mystery, but there it was. "I'm bi." Liam tossed that bit out there as if it were a firecracker. He wanted to see what the man did with the information.

"Oh. Um…" Charlie trailed off for a moment. "Congratulations?"

I deserved that. Liam burst out laughing. "I've been bi since high school, not that I made a big deal of it or anything. I had a boyfriend, and then I had a girlfriend who I married when we were both way too young." He noted the relief on Charlie's face. *Relief that I'm bi? Or relief that I didn't get angry?* he wondered. "Anyway, Portia tells me you're majoring in IT?"

"Graduated, actually," Charlie said, looking bashful again. "I got my master's in process management in an accelerated program, too. So I'm done. I just need to find a good job and pay back all my loans."

"Goodness, that's impressive," Liam said, even more interested in the guy. He was looking for someone to handle the integration of his security and IT systems so he could expand his business into a new location without worrying about technical matters. And if Portia was friends with Charlie, the man wasn't an idiot. His daughter was notoriously picky about her friendships. "Hmm."

"What, hmm?" Charlie asked.

Liam pursed his lips. "I'd like to see your resume." The way he said it sounded suggestive, and he swore internally. What was it about this guy?

Charlie shook his head. "No. No way. I'm not going to go work for my friend's dad."

"What? Why not?" Liam glanced at him. "That's ridiculous. How do you think business works? It's all about networking."

"I know exactly how it works, and I'm not looking for a handout."

Liam chuckled, thinking of the mess that the last guy he'd hired had made, and how much work it would be to fix. "Charlie, believe me, it would *not* be a handout." He eased into the fast lane, speeding up a little. "Besides, I don't even know if your skills would suit the job, because I haven't seen your resume." He glanced at Charlie again. The man was frowning, but he looked merely lost in thought, not belligerent. "It won't hurt to give me your information." He smiled slyly. "Like my daughter said, I don't bite."

Charlie raised an eyebrow. "Yeah, I didn't believe her when she said that, and now that I've met you, I *really* don't believe her."

Is he flirting with me? Be still, my heart. Liam put a hand on his chest. "I'm crushed that you think that." He paused, then continued. "Fine. I bite, but only when asked to."

Charlie laughed, face flushing again. "Okay, fine. You can have a copy of my resume." He pulled out his phone and tapped the display. "There. I emailed a copy to your company."

Interesting. He had my company website at the ready. Liam smiled, pleased. "Excellent." He tilted his head. "You realize I haven't had to work that hard to get a resume in years? I'm out of practice with wooing." If the guy was going to flirt with him, he'd be damned if he wasn't going to flirt *back.* He'd thought Charlie was straight, but perhaps the confusion Portia mentioned hid something the man hadn't faced yet? Charlie looked over at him speculatively, and Liam's cock perked up again. *Down. He's your daughter's friend,* he told it, but the thing had a mind of its own. "Portia never told me that you asked her out," he said, hoping to spur some explanation of the situation.

Charlie sighed, and went back to stroking the leather seat. Liam forced himself to sit still. Watching that finger move back and forth made him want to feel it against his erection, and that didn't particularly help with his good intentions towards daughter's friend. *What happened to your rule about not dating someone two decades younger than you?* he asked himself, wondering if he was heading into an early midlife crisis. *I'm nowhere near midlife though,* he thought as he changed lanes again, just to give himself something constructive to do.

"I haven't had a lot of luck in the dating scene," Charlie finally said.

"Hmm." Liam didn't want to point out that he didn't seem to have any trouble flirting with *him.* No sense in scaring the guy.

"What does that mean?" Charlie asked, a hint of frustration in his voice.

Liam glanced at him, then shrugged. If he asked for it… "Just that you don't seem to have any problem flirting with *me.*"

Charlie looked away. "You're easy to talk to. Maybe it's because I know you're Portia's father. You remind me of her, a little bit."

Liam didn't think that was the entire explanation.

If anything, being Portia's father would make him *more* difficult to flirt with. "Hmm."

"Stop that," Charlie said, voice slipping from soft to peeved. "You keep saying 'hmm' as if that's the answer to everything."

Liam smiled. "I'm trying to be polite." He snorted. "Be grateful. I don't often bother."

"I'm not sure I want you to be polite," Charlie said, unexpectedly.

"That's rather interesting," Liam said slowly, suddenly feeling as though his car had revved up into the redline. "You would like me to be impolite?"

"Maybe I just want a safe way to test out some things," Charlie replied.

"That illuminates precisely nothing," Liam said, although if he were being brutally honest, he had an inkling of what Charlie meant. Except … where in the world did the man get the idea that Liam was *safe*?

"What if I've been pursuing the wrong kind of person all this time?" Charlie asked.

"Wrong as in wrong personality?" Liam prodded. He wasn't going to commit to anything unless Charlie spelled it out. *Wait, I'm not going to commit even if he does spell it out,* he reminded himself. The man was too young, and his daughter's friend, and also… His thoughts trailed off. He didn't have any other reasons. Why was he denying himself this? Charlie was an adult. His daughter set up this damned drive with them because she knew Liam would like him. He ran a hand down his face. *You've just met the guy. Take it easy, Liam.*

"Wrong as in wrong gender," Charlie said, surprising Liam out of his self-imposed mental scolding.

Liam glanced at the man. Charlie wasn't looking at him. He was gripping the edge of the seat as if he was about to fly off of it and crash into something painful.

"And you picked me to try out this new theory of yours?" he asked mildly. He didn't want to frighten Charlie off, after all.

"No." Charlie winced. "I mean, maybe." He looked up at Liam for a brief moment, brown eyes tortured, and then stared straight out through the windshield. "I have no idea, actually. I just know that there's something missing when I go out with women." He sighed. "Portia warned me that you were good at drawing stuff out of people." He laughed softly. "I thought she was being melodramatic, but no. She was right." He ran a hand over his face. "I've only just met you, and here I am, telling you things I've barely admitted to myself."

Portia primed him for me, Liam thought, not sure if he was pleased at his daughter's expert manipulation, or disturbed. He let out the breath he hadn't realized he'd been holding. "Right. Time to stretch our legs," he said, looking for the exit he knew was coming up. As soon as he saw the rest area sign, he inhaled deeply and let it out again, trying to calm his arousal down to something manageable. Just because Charlie suddenly wanted to experiment didn't mean it would go well for either of them. *He could be fooling himself about what he wants,* he thought, easing up the exit ramp to a combination overlook and rest area. He parked facing the highway, surprised that no one else was there, and shut off the car. He listened to the engine tick for a moment, then opened his door and stepped out into the desert heat.

"Shit, I'm sorry," Charlie said, joining him at the stone wall that circled the lot. It was really a nicely designed lookout: the setting sun painted the desert canyons with red and pink. "Just ignore what I said."

"Ignore you? No." Liam shook his head as he leaned on the wall with both hands. "And what are you apologizing for? You haven't done anything." He stared out at the gorgeous view, contemplating his options, and then he turned to the younger man. "I'm not safe, Charlie. I've never been safe." He smiled slowly, taking a bit of the sting out of his words. "However, I'm quite willing to be your experiment."

Charlie swallowed. "I ... what?"

"Experiment. That's what you wanted, yes?" Liam noted that the younger man had jammed his hands into his pockets. Hiding ... what? An erection? *I certainly hope so.* Decision made, Liam stepped forward, crowding Charlie up against the low stone wall. *What's the worst that could happen? You fool around, he learns something about himself, and you've done your daughter's friend a favor,* he told himself as his arousal revved a bit higher. "You realize I shouldn't be doing this," he murmured against Charlie's temple. It took a supreme act of will not to thrust against the younger man.

"Why not?" Charlie whispered. His hands had gone to Liam's hips.

Liam inhaled. Charlie smelled fantastic—a combination of coffee and some unidentifiable woodsy scent—like the guy had recently been standing next to a campfire. "Because you're my daughter's friend. You're at least twenty years younger than me. And because I'm not old enough to have a mid-life crisis yet." He let himself run his hands up Charlie's arms. The solid muscles in his arms appealed to Liam.

"How old are you?" Charlie asked.

Liam went still, surprised by the question. "Thirty-nine." Charlie's biceps felt solid and warm beneath his palms. He resisted the urge to dig his fingers into all of the delicious weight, and kept his touch light. "Old, by your standards."

"That's not old," Charlie said, licking his lips.

"No? What is it then?" Liam tilted his head.

Charlie mirrored him, eyes going dark. "You're mature. Experienced." He slid his hands up Liam's chest. "You're killing me, Liam."

All right then, no more hesitating, Liam thought, leaning in. When his lips touched Charlie's, the younger man sucked in a quick breath. Liam opened his mouth and licked inside.

Chapter Three

"Oh God," Charlie tried to say, but then Liam slid his hands up to the younger man's head, and there was no more room for words. Charlie tasted sweet and smoky, and Liam abruptly knew that he'd just got himself into a deeper bind than he'd anticipated.

I'm not going to be happy with a simple kiss, he thought, even as he pushed harder, pressing his hard-on into Charlie's hip. The younger man moaned, and then Liam threaded his fingers into Charlie's hair, holding his head precisely where he wanted it. "Fuck me," he breathed, biting Charlie's lower lip. "You're dangerous."

"Me? That's ridiculous," Charlie panted, and Liam kissed him again.

"Addicting." Liam mouthed the words against Charlie's jawline. The subtle scratch of whiskers shot a bolt of heat straight through to Liam's cock. It had been *so long* since he'd had the pleasure of another man's beard against his skin. Why the hell had he waited so long? He kissed Charlie again, hands going down to the younger man's ass. Charlie gasped, and his erection pushed into Liam's in the most perfect way.

"Oh my God," Charlie breathed, mouth open against Liam's cheek. "What is this?"

Liam bit Charlie's earlobe. "This is lust," he said, as if that explained everything, but how well he knew that it didn't. He hadn't felt this crazed in years. He thrust once, twice, and then forced himself still. "I want to suck you," he said, kneading Charlie's delectable ass. "I want to make you lose your mind."

Charlie trembled. "Oh."

Liam smiled, then slowly slid down until he was on his knees in front of the younger man. The sunset slanted orange and red across Charlie's body, casting his groin into shadow, but Liam didn't need light for what he was about to do.

"Wait, here? Are you serious?" Charlie asked, biting his lip.

Liam put a hand on the younger man's cock. "Right here. Right now." Truth be told, the risk of getting caught giving head in an interstate rest stop heightened everything. He smirked, then undid Charlie's jeans. The younger man's cock sprang out of his soft boxers, and Liam took him in hand.

"Oh, fuck." Charlie jammed the heel of his hand against his mouth, muffling the rest of his words.

"Easy," Liam murmured, running his lips over Charlie's soft skin. His cock felt silky and hard and delightful against his face, and he opened his mouth to lick the pre-cum welling from the tip. Charlie tasted like smoke and sweetness, and Liam wasted no time sucking him in.

Charlie moaned, hips jerking.

"Go ahead," Liam said, sliding off with a pop that had Charlie grunting. "Fuck my mouth."

Charlie's eyes were dark and shocked as they looked down at him. "I don't want to hurt you."

Liam laughed. "I like pain," he said, taking Charlie in again. When he felt Charlie's erection push against the back of his throat, he relaxed and swallowed.

Charlie shuddered, hands going to Liam's hair. "Oh, fuck, fuck. I can't stop," he muttered, hips moving faster.

Liam hardly had to do a thing. He let Charlie fuck his mouth, swallowing occasionally as long-buried skills came back to life. He hadn't given someone a blowjob in years, but he well remembered how many times he and his first love blew each other. He remembered the way it felt for someone to come completely apart in his arms, and a deep craving for that same connection roared up out of nowhere. He looked up, hoping to find God knew what, and Charlie's expression didn't disappoint. The younger man stared down at him as if Liam were the sun and moon combined. Liam slowly pulled off, rolling Charlie's balls around his palm. "I'm not fragile," he said, voice raspy from the beating his throat was taking. "Let go, Charlie. I'll catch you."

Charlie licked his lips, shaking his head, but then Liam bit him gently. The younger man growled, and shoved back in past Liam's smile, and that was it. His cock jerked, and Liam sucked, swallowing every last drop of Charlie's orgasm. He licked him through it, then slid off and gently tucked him back into his pants.

Charlie panted, hands still in Liam's hair. Liam extracted them and stood up, leaning in. "You taste like danger," he murmured, then kissed him with all of the pent-up longing he'd had no idea he'd been carrying around with him. He wanted to strip the younger man and spread him out on his bed so that he could see every last bit of skin exposed and vulnerable. His own erection was so hard it ached, but Liam wasn't a child. He could deal with a bit of pain if it meant he'd get what he wanted in the end, and he wanted Charlie. He didn't know why or how his libido had suddenly woken up, but it had, and he wasn't the sort of man to deny himself what he craved.

"What the fuck did you just do to me?" Charlie said, gripping Liam by the arms. His eyes were wild.

"I showed you what you wanted," Liam said softly, as if there was no question about what had just happened. *The truth is far more complicated,* he thought, a bit bemused with himself. *It always is.* He kissed Charlie again to shut up the voice inside his head. He had no desire to think about the implications of what he'd just done.

"What about you?" Charlie asked when Liam finally stepped back. The younger man glanced down at the erection Liam knew was firmly pressed up against his jeans, the outline visible to anyone who cared to look. Clearly, Charlie cared, which was a good sign.

Better than him punching me in the face, Liam thought, amused. "What about me?" he asked, nudging Charlie towards the car. The younger man had no idea what he planned, and it was best not to spook the guy.

Charlie chewed on his lip as another car pulled into the rest area and parked. He glanced at the parents and two children that exited, shouting happily, and frowned at Liam. "You can't be comfortable like that."

Liam wasn't, actually, but he had almost two decades on Charlie. He could wait a little longer. "I'm not comfortable, but I like a bit of anticipation." He licked his lower lip, looking at Charlie's mouth. "It whets the appetite."

Charlie swallowed, and Liam recognized the signs of renewed arousal. He smiled, pleased. "Come on, then. Hop in." He got into the driver's side and waited. He wanted Charlie to want him, but he didn't want to pressure him to the point where the younger man felt harassed.

Charlie hesitated for a moment, but then he climbed in and shut the door. "I don't know what the hell just happened," he said again, buckling his seatbelt.

Liam shifted his weight, trying to make a bit more room in his pants, but it didn't really help. "You wondered about yourself. You experimented. What do the results tell you?" he asked as he started the car.

Charlie sighed as he scrubbed his hands through his hair. "That I'm a damned fool."

Liam lifted his eyebrows as he eased back onto

the highway. "A fool? I don't think so."

Charlie looked at him. "No? I just had the most incredible orgasm of my life." He shook his head. "With a guy." He made a sound in the back of his throat. "With my friend's *father,* who I just met today. What the fuck does that say about me?"

Liam pursed his lips, thinking. He didn't want to scare the man off, but he also wasn't a liar. "It says that you finally decided to take that step you always knew was waiting for you, and that step not only didn't kill you, you liked it," he finally said. That didn't sound too threatening, did it? It gave just enough information to Charlie for him to chew on.

Charlie glanced over. "What does that say about you? You didn't have any steps to take."

"Didn't I?" Liam asked mildly. Charlie's frown told him that it wasn't a good enough answer. He tried again. "It says that I know enough about life to seize the good things that come around as soon as I recognize them for the gift that they are."

"You're calling me a gift?" Charlie's small smile eased Liam's worry that he'd stepped too far over the line.

Although, I had the man's dick in my mouth. Technically, I dragged him over the line a half hour ago. Liam shrugged, easing into the fast lane. "Definitely."

Charlie stared at him. "I don't think anyone's ever said that to me before." He tilted his head. "If I'm experimenting, what do you get out of this, though?"

Well, now. That is the million-dollar question, isn't it? Liam asked himself. "Is this really only an experiment for you?"

Charlie's face shut down. "I don't know."

You certainly do know, Liam mused, but he didn't push it. "Don't chew on all the what-ifs so much,

Charlie." He checked the time, and knew that they weren't going to make it to Vegas without stopping again, at least once. He might have made light of his hard-on earlier, but the truth was, he couldn't continue like this indefinitely. He thought his erection would subside, but Charlie had a way of inspiring his lust to new heights. Even the younger man's doubts pinged his libido.

"I'm not concerned with 'what-if'. I'm worried about 'what next'," Charlie said.

"Fair enough," Liam said, thinking about what he wanted to say to this young man who spurred emotions he hadn't felt in years. "You know the idea of *carpe diem*, yes?"

"Of course. Doesn't everyone?" Charlie asked.

Liam smiled. "Perhaps, but not everyone follows the motto. I try to." He took a deep breath, and then did the thing that he always swore he would do, since he was old enough to understand that actions have consequences, but that sometimes the consequences were worth it. He told the truth. "When I first met my boyfriend in high school, we were fourteen. We had no idea what we were doing." He glanced at Charlie. The younger man had shifted to staring out the windshield instead of at the side of Liam's head. "But I didn't question it. I liked him. He liked me. Even then, I knew enough to realize that love like that doesn't happen often." He shrugged. "And I told my parents, and while they weren't happy, they were okay with it."

"So, what happened? Why aren't you still with him?" Charlie asked.

Liam ignored the hard thump in his chest. He knew Charlie would ask. "Neil came out to his parents when we were juniors, and his father threw him out of the house. Neil died on the streets a month later when a gang of good old boys jumped him and beat him to death." Recounting the story, even that succinctly, took care of his erection, at least. He grimaced. "It was a long time ago." He'd have preferred to sport blue balls for the next three hours instead of telling Charlie his history, but needs must, at times. *Charlie already knows life sucks, but he needs to understand that you also have to seize the day.*

Charlie sucked in a hard breath. "Shit. That's fucking awful."

Liam sighed. "Yes, but you already know about awful. I didn't tell you because I wanted you to be afraid. I told you because I learned something really fucking important from Neil's death."

"Not to fall in love?" Charlie asked, clearly trying to deflect the uncomfortable conversation.

He's young, and he's been through a lot, but he still doesn't quite know how to sit in his own skin and own it. Liam glanced over, pinning Charlie with his gaze for a brief second. He could tell the moment Charlie got it by the way his expression tightened. "No. I learned that love is more important than anything, and that it doesn't happen if you don't take risks. I wouldn't trade the couple years I had with Neil for anything in the world. The risk was worth it."

Charlie tapped a finger on his knee. "But then you met Portia's mother. And divorced. So love doesn't always last."

Liam made a face. "I never loved Portia's mother."

"Wait. What?" Charlie sounded surprised.

"I dated Charlotte, and we had fun, but I never intended for her to fall pregnant." Liam remembered well the horror of those days at the tail end of high school. "Her parents wouldn't let her get an abortion, which I think was really difficult for her, but honestly? I was happy to marry her and have Portia. I always wanted kids."

"Portia never said anything about that," Charlie said. "Does she know?"

"She knows that we got married because her grandparents pressured her mother into it. I never lied to my daughter." Liam glanced at his GPS: still a few hours to Vegas. They had time. "I didn't tell her everything when she was young, of course, and I made sure that Portia understood that I was always happy that she was my daughter."

"Wow." Charlie didn't elaborate.

Shocked you, did I? Liam mused, not surprised. "So, the moral of this tale is—"

"Seize the day, because you might be dead tomorrow?" Charlie sounded bitter, and Liam knew he was thinking of his parents.

"No. The moral is that love is the most important emotion in our lives." Liam waited for that to sink in.

"Love isn't that easy," Charlie countered, after a moment.

"True." Liam sighed. "Love isn't easy, but you have to be ready to accept it when it drops into your lap." He wasn't going to come right out and say it, but he could talk around the subject like a pro. *Charlie has no idea that what we felt together is unusual.*

"This doesn't have anything to do with us," Charlie said, sounding sure, as only a twenty-something could.

Liam held back his immediate retort, and changed lanes again. He was taking the next exit off this damned highway regardless of where it led. When he saw the sign, he put on his turn signal.

"What are you doing? Vegas is at least two more

hours from here," Charlie said.

"I need to rest my eyes for a moment," Liam said. He wasn't exactly lying; he simply wasn't telling the whole truth.

"I can drive," Charlie said.

"I was hoping you'd say that," Liam took the exit, and then drove for a bit before pulling off the side of the road. They were in the middle of nowhere in the desert. Around them sat nothing but darkness and scrub and rocky ground. He got out of the car and walked around to the passenger's side.

Charlie got out and shut the door, but Liam made no move to get back in. "Stretching your legs?" Charlie asked.

Liam looked at the younger man. *Do I really want to do this? I literally just met him a few hours ago.* He thought of his daughter talking about Charlie over the last several months, and a feeling of *hmm* came over him. "Did Portia talk to you about me?"

Charlie looked startled. "She talked about you all the time, man."

The little minx. She's matchmaking. Liam snorted as several pieces of insight happened to fall into place in his mind, like a puzzle putting itself together. "My daughter is a very intelligent woman." He smiled. "She takes after me, of course."

Charlie frowned at that. "What are you getting at?"

Instead of answering, Liam walked closer to the younger man. "What did she say about me?" He had a feeling that his darling daughter hadn't been dwelling on his fatherly features when she talked about him to Charlie.

Charlie looked away. "She mentioned how busy you always were. She mentioned that more than once, actually."

"And?" Liam drew the word out.

"And she said she thought were lonely, because you never made time to meet anyone." Charlie shrugged. "She said that a lot, actually. I think she worries about you." He cocked his head. "Are you?"

"Lonely?" Liam asked. Inside, he was equal parts disgruntled and proud. His daughter had set him up perfectly. "Yes. Sometimes." He leaned back against the car. The cool air of the desert smelled fresh, belying the arid hopelessness of the hot day. "My dear daughter told me that she thought you needed someone older, who understood what you'd been through, Charlie."

Charlie laughed. "She said that?"

Liam nodded.

"Huh." Charlie leaned back against the car next to Liam. "What's going on here, Liam?"

Liam grinned. "My daughter played matchmaker for us. And she did a damned good job of it."

Chapter Four

Charlie stared at him. Even in the dark Liam could see the younger man's disbelief, clear as day, on his face.

"You don't believe me," Liam said, not that it mattered. Belief or disbelief didn't preclude the facts.

"I think it's unlikely," Charlie said.

Liam's gaze raked down Charlie's body, and all of his instincts sat up and told him *yes, this is real.* "It's not unlikely at all, my dear," he murmured, moving closer. His cock twitched, and the erection he'd lost earlier slowly came back to life.

Charlie didn't budge. "Why would she set me up with you?"

"Because I taught *her* to seize the day," Liam said, amused all over again that his daughter had taken the motto and changed it to suit her needs. *And her need right now is to make her father happy.* "She knew I'd like you. She made sure to tell me about you so I wouldn't feel as though you were a stranger when we finally met." He touched Charlie's cheek lightly. "And she made certain you would feel kindly disposed towards me."

"That's … manipulative." Charlie shook his head. "No. Portia isn't that kind of person."

Liam laughed. "Portia totally *is* that kind of person, when it comes to getting something she wants, and she seems to want to make us happy." He remembered the year she'd decided she wanted to learn how to drive a manual transmission and somehow managed to talk him into letting her drive his Porsche— all so she could improve her "life skills". The summer of her sixteenth birthday had been delightful, actually. He dismissed the memory. He didn't want to think about his daughter right now. He wanted to seduce Charlie. He put his hands on the roof of the car on either side of the younger man's shoulders. "Admit it. You've been curious about me for a while, yes?"

Charlie licked his lips. "Perhaps."

Liam snorted, and leaned in to kiss him. "My daughter set us up, Charlie."

"That's crazy." Charlie's lips twitched.

"It's the truth." Liam pressed in, reveling in the softness of Charlie's mouth. "I've been tired of working so much lately. I want to fall in love." He nibbled on Charlie's lips. "And here you are."

"Love? In one day? That's impossible," Charlie protested, but his mouth opened to let Liam in. His hands moved from the car to Liam's shoulders.

"Being in love won't happen in one day, but falling in love can," Liam said, slotting his thigh between Charlie's legs. He wanted to strip the man naked and fuck him right here, right now. "Ever given any thought to anal sex?"

Charlie shuddered. "You can't be serious?"

"Oh, I'm deadly serious," Liam said, licking into Charlie's neck. He gently bit down on the tendon leading to his shoulder. "Imagine my finger sliding into you, pressing up against your prostate. My mouth on your cock felt good. This would feel even better."

"How—" Charlie broke off, gasping for air as Liam slid his hands around to grip his ass. "How can you make that sound appealing?"

"Because it is." Liam unbuckled the younger man's pants. "The car is the perfect height for it." He cupped Charlie's cock. "I'm dying to fuck you."

Charlie moaned, head thrown back. "What about lube? Isn't that sort of important? And we're in the middle of nowhere."

Liam slid his hand down to press up behind Charlie's balls. "I have lube. I have condoms." He didn't lie. He always carried some, not that he'd had opportunity to use them in the past few years. He simply liked to be prepared. He fingered Charlie's tight hole, smiling against his skin as the man's hips jerked. "I can be so deep inside you that you wouldn't remember your name. And I'm not nice enough to back down now that I know what you feel like against my body."

"Oh, God," Charlie gasped, hands tightening painfully on Liam's arms. "What if someone sees us?"

Liam lifted his head and looked around. The desert looked back at them, quiet and dark. "There isn't anyone around for miles. Even the highway is quiet."

Charlie swallowed. "I can't believe I'm considering this."

Liam stepped back. "Don't move."

Charlie laughed. "I can't move. If I tried, I'd fall down." He touched himself, shivering as his hand gripped his cock.

Liam forced himself to look away before he lost all control. "Just a moment." He opened the door and popped the glovebox, grabbing a condom and a small packet of lube. He placed them on top of the car, then shrugged out of his shirt. "You sure about this?"

Charlie shook his head. "No."

Liam nodded. "You will be."

Charlie watched him undo his pants and kicked off his shoes. The gravel of the road bit into his feet, but Liam didn't give a fuck. "Off," he said, pulling Charlie's t-shirt up and over his head.

"This is insane."

Liam smiled. "All the best things in life are." He splayed his hands on Charlie's delicious pecs, then reached down and pulled his jeans off. "Up with you."

Charlie sat up on the hood, cock bobbing.

Liam opened the condom and rolled it on his cock, then tore open the packet of lube. "Breathe," he said.

Charlie snorted. "This is awkward." He looked like a man on the edge of running away: long limbs splayed and hair askew, but it was the hesitation in his eyes that truly worried Liam.

He'll settle down, he thought, moving closer. "Not for long, it won't be," he said. He cupped Charlie's erection, then stretched the younger man out on the hood of his Land Rover, as if screwing hot young men out in the desert was something he did every other day. *And the truth is, I haven't done this in years,* he thought, even as his slick thumb found Charlie's hole and teased at the muscles.

Charlie quivered, and Liam smiled as he leaned down to lick along the younger man's erection. "Oh God," Charlie said, voice going low and shocked.

"I'm not God," Liam said, then sucked lightly. When Charlie began pushing up into his mouth, he slid a finger inside. The younger man whined, hips snapping up, and Liam deep throated him.

"Fuck, fuck," Charlie said, writhing on the hood of the car.

"Another," Liam said, licking down to Charlie's balls. He inserted another finger, and then another. "Breathe," he said again, as Charlie's grimaced.

"It burns," he said, but his erection hadn't wilted.

"That burn will feel good in a moment," Liam assured him. He sucked on the head of Charlie's cock, screwing his fingers deeper. He waited for the young man to groan, and then he crooked his middle finger, searching for the spot he knew would push the younger man from acceptance into need.

"Oh!" Charlie almost came off the hood as Liam slid off his cock, smiling.

"Found it," he murmured, as Charlie suddenly fucked down on his fingers.

"Oh Jesus, don't stop." Charlie reached up and grabbed Liam's shoulders, hips pressing harder. "God. Please."

Liam moved closer, then pulled out so he could spread more lube on his sheathed cock. Charlie moaned a protest, but Liam was quick. "Breathe," he said again as he placed his erection right up against Charlie's hole.

"Stop saying that," Charlie snarled, hips jerking.

Liam gritted his teeth and circled Charlie's erection with his slick fingers. "You want me?"

Charlie nodded, sweat slicking his hair. "I can't believe I'm saying this, but yes. Come on."

Liam slowly pushed inside as Liam's entire body tensed up. "Push down," he said, hissing as the younger man's body resisted him.

Charlie groaned, and then suddenly, Liam slipped inside. The insane heat of it almost tipped him over the edge. He hadn't fucked another man in over twenty years, no matter what his damned ex-wife believed of him. "Fuck," he muttered, panting as his control nearly shattered.

"Come on. Move," Charlie said, hips trying to push down on Liam's cock.

"Give me a minute," Liam said through gritted teeth. He squeezed Charlie's cock, counting in his head until he came down a bit from the edge. "All right. Now, where were we?" he asked, rolling his hips. He knew the angle he wanted, and sure enough, when Charlie cried out, he knew he'd got it right on the first try.

"Oh my God," Charlie grabbed his shoulders, shivering as he arched his spine. "There. Right fucking there."

Liam smiled grimly, and pulled out, ignoring Charlie's whine of protest. Before the younger man could move, he pushed back in, and then did it again, hitting his prostate with each thrust. Charlie started to shake, and Liam began to stroke his cock in time with his thrusts. "Come on, Charlie. Come for me."

Charlie whipped his head back and forth. "Oh fuck."

"Yes, that's it," Liam said, riding the edge again. "Come on." He palmed Charlie's cock, almost too far gone to manage anything else, and then the younger man's orgasm squeezed his erection, and he couldn't do a damned thing except fuck him and fuck him until the pleasure swept him up, too. He thrust in, hard, and held it there as Charlie's climax pushed him over, and the scent of sex and semen and the desert barreled through him in an unforgettable rush. His hips jerked forward, and he groaned, leaning down over Charlie as everything in his life narrowed into a single, incandescent point. The younger man held on to him as if they'd both fly apart if he let go, and for a strange moment, Liam was grateful that it had happened this way, because he couldn't imagine anything else more perfect right now.

"Liam," Charlie whispered, and Liam kissed him quiet, before he said something he'd never be able to take back.

Before I say something I can't take back, he thought, inhaling and exhaling very carefully until he felt as though his body was all right, and wouldn't collapse at a moment's notice. "You're okay," he said, patting Charlie's shoulder, and the younger man gave him a disbelieving look. *Right. I deserved that. Because falling in love in the middle of the desert on top of my car is so totally normal,* Liam thought, shocked at himself for losing all sense of restraint, but then Charlie sighed and went boneless and Liam had to pry his fingers away from the younger man's skin. He didn't want to, but his fingers ached, and so did his heart. He didn't regret a moment of it. "Charlie," he said, licking suddenly dry lips. "Are you okay?"

Charlie laughed, short and soft. "I don't know."

Liam knew precisely what he meant. "Hmm," he said, swallowing the dust and shoving his uncertainty down to where it wouldn't interfere with what he had to say. He pulled out slowly, wincing a little. Charlie had been tight, and if *he* was sore, the younger man had to be feeling the sting even more. He took care of the condom, and then he helped Charlie down from the hood. The younger man slung an arm over Liam's shoulders, pulling him into an embrace, and they stood like that for a long time.

"We're a mess," Charlie finally said.

Liam nodded. "Indeed."

"I don't know if I care." Charlie took a shaky step away, and then made a face at the mess on his abdomen.

"Hang on," Liam said, grabbing some tissues from inside the car. He handed a pile of them to Charlie, then swabbed at himself. After a futile attempt to clean up, he gave up, and pulled his pants on over the carnage. When he looked up, Charlie had already zipped up his jeans. He looked … wrecked. *Oh, I'm in so much trouble,* Liam thought, wondering how the hell he was going to let this man go. Charlie was everything he'd ever wanted, but he was so fucking young.

"So, what now?" Charlie asked.

"Now?" Liam licked his lips. "Now, we get you to Vegas," he said, knowing already that merely dropping Charlie off wouldn't be enough for him. *I'm not going to let him go unless he makes me,* he thought, even as his rational mind urged him to play it cool.

"And that's it? You drop me off, and we go our separate ways?"

No, Liam thought, but he didn't say the word out loud. "Get in." He tempered his terse command with a smile. Charlie's expression eased a bit. "I'm not going to do anything you don't want to do, Charlie," he added, opening the door. He waited as Charlie gathered up the rest of his clothes and tossed them inside. Once the younger man had settled into the passenger's seat, Liam put on his shoes and got in the car. "You're my daughter's friend."

"That's a cop out," Charlie said quietly. "I'm a hell of a lot more than Portia's friend, now."

Liam carefully exhaled, and started the car. "Give me your phone."

Charlie quirked an eyebrow at him.

Liam held out his hand. Charlie sighed and gave him his cell phone. Liam quickly opened up his contacts list and added his number. "Call me anytime, day or night."

Charlie frowned, then tapped the icon. Liam's phone rang, but he ignored it, waiting for Charlie to cut the connection.

"Now you have my number, too," Charlie said, as if he didn't expect Liam to want it. He slid his phone back into his pocket.

"Good," Liam said, wondering how long he'd be able to stay away. *You need to give him space,* he reminded himself, though he wasn't sure Charlie knew that.

"You think this happened too fast," Charlie said a few moments later.

Liam nodded, easing back onto the interstate. "Didn't it?"

"Maybe." Charlie frowned. "I don't know." He sighed, rubbing his eyes. "I feel like I've known you for months."

"Because of Portia," Liam said, thinking about his daughter's sly campaign to find him a boyfriend. He smiled. He'd been well and truly played. *I should never have taught her how to gamble.*

"Yeah." Charlie looked out the window. "But I also feel really fucking confused. I never knew sex could feel like that."

"You were dating the wrong gender," Liam pointed out.

"I guess." Charlie sounded reluctant to admit it.

Liam pressed his lips together, contemplating the almost twenty years of distance he had over Charlie. He already knew who *he* was, but his lover was still trying to figure himself out. "It takes as long as it takes, Charlie. You can't rush it."

"We're not talking about my sexuality, are we?" Charlie asked.

Liam shrugged.

Charlie glared at him. "Give me a break, Liam. I just lost my virginity to you."

Liam glanced at the younger man. "I know," he said softly. He was starting to see signs for Las Vegas. It wouldn't be much longer before they arrived at Charlie's aunt and uncle's house. He reached out and put his hand on Charlie's forearm. "I know," he said, more forcefully.

Charlie tensed, as if to shrug him off, but then he turned his arm over and threaded their fingers together. "I'm sorry."

Liam smiled. "It's okay."

"I don't know why I'm being so cranky." Charlie tightened their grip. "I'm not normally like this."

Because you're feeling vulnerable and confused

and exhausted, all at the same time, Liam thought, feeling all those things, too, and more. "It's late," he said aloud as he pulled into the fast lane. It was time to get Charlie home, and get himself the hell away from the man so they could both think about what they'd done without falling all over each other again. Liam had always been one for ripping off a bandage all at once. He hated when people picked at the damned things for three days. "Call me," he said again. "Any time. I'll be there."

"You really think it will go that badly?" Charlie asked. "I'm just going to come out to my family, not admit I'm a serial killer."

Liam lifted a shoulder. "I honestly have no idea." There. There was the exit. His phone map alerted him just as he switched lanes again.

"You have my number, too," Charlie said quietly.

Liam took the next exit and smoothly decelerated. "I do."

"Take the next right," Charlie said, tapping Liam's phone to cancel the GPS app. "I'd rather just tell you which way to go."

"Not one for machine prompting?" Liam asked, taking the turn a little too sharply.

Charlie smiled wryly. "Why follow directions when you already know the way home?"

"Because maybe there's a new way out that you didn't know was there," Liam said. Charlie stared at him so long, and so intently, that Liam almost pulled over to shake him until he grew up. "Relax. Not everything is a metaphor," Liam finally said.

"Fine." Charlie stared out the window, a slight frown marring his forehead. "Turn here." Charlie pointed. "It's the last house on the left."

Liam slowed the car, noting the neat natural landscaping in the front yard. *Stones and spiky plants.*

Not very welcoming. He sighed quietly to himself. Other peoples' life choices were not his responsibility. "Are you going to be all right?"

Charlie undid his seatbelt as Liam pulled into the driveway. "I'll be fine."

"You did just have a hell of a revelation." Liam shut the car off.

"Yeah, well, better late than never," Charlie said wryly. "And I'm a grown man, remember?" His hand slid down his thigh, drawing Liam's gaze to his considerable assets. "I'll survive."

Fuck, Liam thought as his cock stirred. He watched Charlie get out and grab his bag. "Bloody hell," he muttered, getting out, too. "Charlie," he called, before the younger man could walk up the sidewalk. Charlie waited as Liam walked around the car, and the younger man's face told him that he was already steeling himself for what he had to do. "Survival is all well and good, but people need more."

Charlie's expression softened. "You gave me more."

Liam reached out and pulled the younger man into a hug. "I'll give you more than the hood of a car if you'll let me." There. He hadn't said everything he meant, but he'd said part of it. Enough for Charlie to have something to hold onto.

Charlie nodded. "That's … good." He cleared his throat. "Good to know."

Liam nodded, too, and then he stepped back. "I'll see you later." He'd be damned if he would say goodbye.

"Later." Charlie lifted a hand, and then he turned and headed up the walk.

Liam got back in the car, and pulled out of the driveway, just as Charlie opened the door to the house. He didn't wait to see if Charlie's family was there. He didn't watch the door close.

Chapter Five

"Dad, you're being completely absurd. You know that, right?" Portia said. Her exasperation came through loud and clear, despite the terrible connection. "Just call him. When the hell did you turn into a girl? Man up and pick up the phone."

I already have, and he didn't answer. Liam scowled down at his phone. His daughter wasn't normally so salty. "Portia, it's only been a week. And your friend has a lot on his mind right now." At least, that's what he told himself every time Charlie ignored his texts.

"Give me a break. I can tell you've been moping around even from Hawaii." Static obscured the rest of her words.

"I'm not moping, Portia. I'm biding my time," Liam said. So what if he'd texted her more than once? She was his daughter, after all. He wanted her to be happy. He was just checking in with her.

"You asked me about Charlie every day this week." Portia snorted. "And like I told you on Tuesday, I only heard from him once, on Monday. He said you guys hit it off." Her sigh told him precisely how frustrated he was making her. "I don't know what more you want from me. An engraved invitation? The ball is in your court now."

Liam glared at the wall of his office. She had a point. He'd tried calling, but he *could* always drive out to Charlie's aunt and uncle's house. *Although wouldn't that be veering into stalker territory?*

"Dad? You there? This connection is terrible," his daughter said. "Did you hear what I said?"

"I still can't believe you set me up with him," Liam said instead of answering her question. He tapped at the top of his desk, trying to relieve his nervous energy. The bank of security monitors over on the right wall flipped from room to room, overseeing the customers just beginning to file into his luxury nightclub. "Look, darling, I love you, but I need to go. Work calls."

"You should be calling Charlie," Portia said, but then she sighed again. "You know I love you, too, Dad."

Liam smiled faintly. She could never stay irritated with him for long. "I'll talk to you tomorrow," he said, but she cut him off before he could say more.

"No, you won't. You'll talk to me next week. It's time to cut the cord," she told him.

Liam had to laugh. "Have I really been that bad?"

She snorted. "Yes, you have. I love you. I'm hanging up now."

"I love you, too, Portia," he said, and then he tapped the screen of his phone, cutting the connection before she yelled at him some more. "Takes after me," he muttered, knowing he had no one to blame but himself for her attitude. His ex was quietly manipulative. He far preferred Portia's more direct methods.

"Liam? We've got a situation," James, Liam's security chief, said from the doorway of the office.

Liam frowned, looking at the bank of monitors. He didn't see anything amiss. "What is it?"

James stepped into the room and tapped the switch that brought up the front door's screen. Liam didn't usually monitor that one because he employed two bouncers for the front door. He focused on the scene, then stood up. Two men were shoving another guy wearing a hoodie. His bouncers were holding back two others. "Send more guys."

"Arnie and Jack aren't here yet. Traffic," James said apologetically. "The situation isn't out of hand yet. I came to let you know about it as soon as I saw it."

Liam cursed, already heading for the door. "Come on."

"I called the cops," James said as he followed Liam.

"Good." Liam took the stairs, not willing to wait for the elevator. James followed him down and through the club. When they reached the front door, Liam stood for a moment to assess the situation, and then his blood ran cold. The men were shouting homophobic slurs. Anger surged through him, but he knew he had to remain calm. "Idiots," he muttered under his breath, and then he waded into the fray. He grabbed the arm of the man about to deck the guy being harassed. He still couldn't get a good look at the victim because of the crowd, not that it mattered. He wasn't going to put up with this shit. "If you think gay bashing is okay in my club, you're quite mistaken," he snarled as he hauled the attacker back, beyond pissed that anyone would dare be so stupid on *his* property. His club was well known as an all-inclusive space for queer people of all stripes, as well as straights. "My club is called The Queer Speakeasy for a reason, fool."

"Fuck you! You're not the boss of me," the man yelled, turning on Liam. "Are you a faggot, too?"

Liam rolled his eyes. "Actually, I'm bi, not that it matters." He turned to James. "How long for the cops?"

"Two minutes," James said, holding back the third man.

The guy Liam had yanked back growled and lifted his free arm. "I wouldn't do that if I were you," Liam said, twisting the arm he still held higher up the man's back. He glanced over, nodding as he saw that his bouncers still had the man's friends under control. "Just a moment, folks, and we'll open the doors," he said to the waiting line of club-goers.

"Cocksucker," the guy hissed, struggling.

Really, why doesn't anyone come up with a more original insult? Liam groused silently. "Yes, yes, I *am* a cocksucker. You should try it. It might improve your disposition," Liam said, unable to resist being flippant. "Lots of vitamins and minerals in semen, you know." The giggles from the crowd told him that he'd succeeded in diffusing a lot of the tension, at least for them. The guy and his friends weren't amused, because the man hissed, trying to lunge towards him, but Liam held him easily." You realize your arm will pop right out of your shoulder socket if you keep this up," he said, growing more irritated by the minute. First his daughter called to yell at him, and now this. He really just wanted a vacation, preferably with Charlie, definitely somewhere quiet, and, he hoped, with a bed. From the corner of his eye, he saw his two tardy bouncers rushing up the sidewalk to help. *Thank goodness. I'm liable to break this man's arm out of annoyance.* He eased up a bit on his hold. He didn't need a lawsuit on top of everything else.

"Liam."

What— Liam froze, then let go of the man's arm. One of the bouncers smoothly stepped up and took over before the man could deck him. Liam turned, dismissing the idiot from his mind while he focused on the voice. Was he hearing things?

"Charlie?" he asked, and then, as if he'd conjured the younger man out of thin air, his lover stood in front of him, hair mussed and with a darkening bruise decorating his cheek. The neckline of his dark blue hoodie was stretched out as if someone had yanked on it.

"Yeah, it's me," Charlie said, smiling.

"What the hell?" Liam grabbed him and pulled him into a hug. "You don't answer my calls or texts and now you just show up?" He leaned back, taking in the bruise on his face. "Dammit." He touched the skin carefully, then fingered his hoodie. Charlie must have been the guy those jokers were harassing.

"I'm fine. He got in a lucky throw," Charlie said, wincing when Liam's fingers went back to the bruise. "Easy."

Liam lightened his touched. "You can certainly press charges for this." The complex mix of emotions roiling his gut didn't help him get control of his anger over those homophobic fools.

"No." Charlie shook his head. "I'm not in the mood to deal with that. Not after this hellish week."

What happened to him? Liam wondered, taking in Charlie's exhaustion. "I'm going to make you pay for not returning my calls," he said, pulling the younger man into a hug. He kissed the bruise, then Charlie's lips. "I thought you ghosted me," he said against his mouth. Dimly, he heard the crowd people in line clapping. If he weren't so busy kissing Charlie, he'd roll his eyes at the lot of them.

Charlie shook his head. "No, never. My phone died when my uncle threw it at me. Shattered the screen. I couldn't access my contacts list because then it didn't sync with my computer properly." He sighed. "It took a few days for me to pull my shit together." He glanced around. "You never told me the name of your club. I had to ask Portia." He smiled wryly. "That was Monday. Or was it Tuesday?" He huffed under his breath. "I can't keep track of the days anymore. I spent half of the week extracting my belongings from their house, and finding a car."

"Bloody hell." Liam could just imagine why Charlie's uncle had thrown his phone at him.

"So, I'm kind of homeless at the moment,"

Charlie continued.

"Homeless?" Liam blinked, then grabbed him. "Can you mop up, James?" he tossed over his shoulder.

James smirked at him while he held onto a sullen looking teen. "Sure thing, Boss," he said, somehow sounding both amused and badass.

Of course these idiots would be teens, Liam thought, irritated at the situation all over again. "You're coming with me," he told Charlie. "You're *not* homeless."

"Where are we going?" Charlie didn't resist at all as Liam dragged him into the club.

"Your new home, of course." Liam headed straight for the elevators. "I looked at your resume, you know. You're hired."

Charlie laughed. "Just like that?"

The elevator door opened, and Liam pushed him inside, and then crowded him up against the back wall. "No, not just like that." He grabbed Charlie's arms as the doors shut. "I'm angry and worried and so fucking relieved, you have no idea," he said, kissing the younger man again. Charlie made a sound somewhere between pained and desperate, and Liam gentled his kiss.

"I'm sorry," Charlie said softly.

"I was about to head out to your house," Liam said, resting his forehead on the younger man's. "I decided to drag you back to me kicking and screaming if I had to."

Charlie laughed bitterly. "I wasn't there. On Monday, when you drove me, I was too tired to say anything to my aunt and uncle. I came out to them on Tuesday." He grimaced. "It didn't go well."

"I would've helped," Liam began, but Charlie was already shaking his head.

"No need. I'm a grownup. I had a feeling they'd

react like that."

Liam sighed. "I still would've helped."

"I know," Charlie said with a soft smile.

The elevator doors opened, and Liam nudged the younger man into his penthouse. "Welcome home, Charlie."

Charlie looked around, wide eyed at the expanse of glass and marble and Vegas view. "You mean that."

"Of course." Liam took Charlie's battered bag from him and dropped it on the glass coffee table. "I know you're young, and I know you probably have a lot to figure out right now, but I'm staring down the frontside of middle age and I don't have the time."

Charlie pulled off his hoodie and tossed it on Liam's leather sofa. "I figured a lot out over the past few days. I'm not confused, and I don't really give a damn that you're old."

Liam snorted. "I'm older than you, not *old*."

Charlie grinned, and Liam nearly winced as the expression twisted the bruise on the younger man's face. That shit had to hurt.

"Are you saying you're too old for me?" Charlie asked.

Liam caught up to him in three quick strides. "Never."

"Good." Charlie's grin relaxed into a smile that seized Liam's heart and didn't let go. "Because I'd like to stay."

"Good," Liam said, kissing him softly. "Because I'm not letting you leave again." He touched Charlie's face. "Maybe you should see a doctor."

"Hell to the no," Charlie said, shaking his head emphatically. "The guy got in a lucky shot. It's sore, but my head doesn't hurt. I'm fine."

Liam sighed. "I'm not letting you out of my sight

for at least a day. Maybe longer." The last thing he wanted was for Charlie to collapse from an undiagnosed concussion.

"Relax. I'm okay." Charlie threaded his fingers through Liam's hair and tugged gently. "It's just a little bruise."

Liam let him. Charlie could do whatever the hell he wanted with him, now and forever. He sighed, relaxing as the last vestiges of anger slid into the slow burn of arousal. That was a much better emotion to stoke.

"This is kind of insane, you realize that?" Charlie said, fingers going from Liam's hair to the buttons on his shirt.

"Love at first sight," Liam said, thinking of his daughter. She had been right about Charlie. She was never going to let him live this down. He looked at the younger man. The word *love* didn't seem to faze him, thank God.

"Portia is going to torment us about this for the rest of our lives," Charlie said, echoing Liam's thoughts.

Liam made a face. "Let's not talk about my daughter while you're undressing me, hmm?"

Charlie laughed. "Good point." By now he had Liam's shirt halfway down his arms. "Your club can run itself for a night, right?"

Liam nodded as he sank his fingers into the waistband of Charlie's jeans. "It can run itself for the rest of the week, for all I care, love."

"There's that word again," Charlie murmured, taking off his shirt.

Liam smiled and undid the top button of Charlie's jeans. He could feel his lover's cock pressing insistently against the fabric. "I don't want to waste time."

Charlie swallowed, then pulled Liam's shirt off the rest of the way. "I hear you."

Liam didn't need Charlie to say the word back to him. He could see the younger man's emotions in the way that he looked at him, he could feel them in how he touched Liam's skin, and he knew damned well that Charlie's heart was just as full and just as vulnerable as his. He didn't need to say it out loud. "I'm going to suck you off, and then you're going to fuck me," he said instead.

Charlie shuddered. "No."

Liam paused. "No?" He knew Charlie wasn't pushing him away, because he was literally pulling him closer.

"No, I can't wait for that." Charlie's hands slid into Liam's slacks and curled around his erection so perfectly that he groaned, abruptly on the edge.

"Fuck," Liam said, skin tingling. He dropped his head onto Charlie's shoulder and concentrated on simply breathing, but the scent of Charlie's skin only made him want him more.

"Come on." Charlie slid away, looking around. "There has to be a bed here somewhere."

Liam closed his eyes for a moment, trying to get himself under control. "This way," he said roughly, when he thought he could walk without climaxing in his pants like a teenager. He led the way to his bedroom. Charlie didn't look at the gleaming furniture or the stainless-steel appliances in the kitchen. He didn't stop to ask questions about the penthouse, or his new job. He followed Liam to the bed, and stripped his clothes off with ruthless efficiency. Liam watched him, mouth going dry, then hurriedly did the same. When they were both naked, Charlie pushed him down onto the bed.

"I can't wait," he said, climbing on top.

Liam arched his back, gasping when their cocks slid across each other. "Neither can I."

Charlie's hips undulated, and Liam pressed his fingers into the skin of his lover's ass. He remembered how perfect it had felt to fuck him, and how surprised he had been that Charlie let him. "We've only known each other for a week," he gasped.

Charlie bit down on his shoulder. "A week, a year, what the hell difference does it make?"

And therein lies the heart of the matter, Liam thought, but then Charlie wrapped his hand around both their cocks and he couldn't really think anymore at all. He groaned, hips moving faster.

"Yeah, that's it," Charlie said, voice dark and low, and Liam realized that he'd stopped thinking of Charlie as too young sometime right before the man had pushed him on the bed.

"Fuck," Liam said, close to coming.

"Next time," Charlie replied, squeezing tighter— almost too tightly. He was firmly in the driver's seat, and Liam loved it, even as his cock told him that the little bit of pain was almost too much. He gasped, debating internally with himself, and then he reached down and eased Charlie's hand away.

"I told you I wanted you to fuck me," he said, rolling over to grab lube and condoms from the bedside table. "I want you to know how it feels."

Charlie whined, clearly frustrated. "Are you serious? After this week, you're going to make me go slow?"

Liam turned back to him, grinning wickedly. "Who said anything about slow?" He uncapped the bottle of lube and spread a generous amount over Charlie's cock.

Charlie's hips jerked, but Liam held him down. "Easy."

"Easy? Easy for you to say," Charlie retorted, but

by then Liam had the condom out and was rolling it down over his lover's erection. Charlie shuddered, and Liam could feel just how close he was.

"You'll like this," Liam promised as Charlie glared at him. He smiled, loving the new cranky Charlie. "Watch." Liam drew his legs back and fingered himself, making sure to get himself nice and slick. It had been decades since he'd been on the receiving end of things, and he knew it would be a bit of a shock to his system. He wanted to be ready so that Charlie didn't have to be gentle.

"Oh my fucking God, what the hell are you doing?" Charlie asked. He had a hand around his cock, and Liam could tell he was squeezing hard in an attempt to control himself.

"What does it look like I'm doing?" Liam asked, going breathy as he added another finger. His muscles were tight, but he was damned motivated. Bottoming might not be something he wanted to do often, but for Charlie, he'd give it a go.

"Oh, fuck," Charlie said, going up on his knees.

Liam leaned back further, knowing that the sight of his fingers entering his body was filthy, and that Charlie loved it. "Come on, Charlie. Fuck me."

Charlie moaned, then moved forward and grabbed Liam's arm, easing his fingers out. "I don't know what the fuck I'm doing here." He put the tip of his cock at Liam's entrance.

Liam pulled him in, breathing out as the head of Charlie's cock pushed at his hole. "It's not that hard, love."

Charlie went still, then snorted. "I can't believe you said that." He stared down at Liam, eyes bright as he tried to hold back a smile.

Liam laughed. "I couldn't resist." He wrapped his

legs around Charlie's waist. "Fuck me."

Charlie groaned, and then his hips were pushing forward. "I'm not going to last."

Liam breathed out as the most delicious sensation filled him. Charlie's cock inside his body felt hot and hard and perfect. "You don't have to," he managed to say, and then Charlie pulled out and shoved back in, face tight with pleasure. "Ah, God. You're fucking perfect, Charlie."

Charlie shook his head, even as his hips moved faster, and then faster again. "You're the one who's perfect," he said, voice gone low. He shifted his weight, and that changed the angle of his thrusts. Liam's smile slipped away as Charlie's cock hit his prostate, and he cried out as pleasure fractured any ability he had to form words.

"Oh, yeah, that's fucking—" Charlie broke off, eyes closed tightly.

Liam held on, groaning as the heat built. Charlie growled, pumping harder, and then Liam's climax pushed through him like the deep bass of a massive club song. He groaned, cock jerking as he orgasmed without anyone even touching him. Charlie echoed him as he followed Liam down into pleasure.

A long time later, Charlie heaved himself off of Liam and sprawled out on the bed. "Hell."

Liam smiled, too fucked to even wipe himself off. The mess they'd made was going to dry all over him and be a bitch to deal with later, but he didn't care. "Not hell, heaven."

Charlie snorted. "You're such a sap."

"Only for you, Charlie," Liam said, smirking. "And you'd better not tell anyone."

"Or what?" Charlie rolled onto his side and went up on his elbow.

Liam smiled at his lover. Charlie's brown hair was going eight different directions and the bruise on his chin had darkened a bit, but his brown eyes were bright and happy. "Or I'll tell Portia you're being cruel to me. She'll handle you."

Charlie's eyes widened in mock horror. "You wouldn't dare."

Liam lifted an eyebrow in response, and Charlie burst out laughing. After he caught his breath, he leaned over and kissed Liam gently. "I really hope she doesn't go all weird on me for moving in with you."

"Love, she's probably going to throw us a party," Liam told him, pulling him down and tucking him against his side. "She's been after me to start dating again for years."

"She's been throwing hints at me about meeting you for a while." Charlie shook his head. "I think she knew I was gay before I did."

"She's an insightful woman," Liam said.

"She told me that her mom left because you were bi." Charlie's voice held a hint of questioning.

Liam sighed. "Yes. I met Charlotte in high school, after Neil died. I'd switched schools, and no one there knew I'd once dated a boy. She hit on me, I let things happen, and the next thing I knew, she fell pregnant at the tail end of our senior year. Her parents forced us to get married." He shook his head. "I was young, and stupid, but I don't regret it. Portia is one of the best things that ever happened to me."

"You didn't tell your ex you were bi?"

"I mentioned it, but I believe she thought I was trying to be hip. I didn't pursue it because the point was moot. I was married to her. What did it matter that I also found men attractive?" He absently rested his cheek on Charlie's shoulder. "I should've explained it better to her, but then we had a baby to take care of. She found the pictures of Neil and me one day when we were visiting my parents. She lost it."

"That's awful," Charlie said in a hushed voice.

Liam shrugged. "I wasn't as broken up about the divorce as I could've been, but then, I never really fell in love with her properly." He smiled wryly. "Maybe I only truly fall in love with men. Who knows?"

After a moment, Charlie let out a long breath. "I don't think I'm bi, Liam."

Liam smiled. "It wouldn't matter to me if you were."

"I know." Charlie went up on an elbow again. "Are you sure you want to take me on?" He looked around the bedroom, gaze lingering on the high-end dresser Liam had put near the window. "You could have anyone, you know." His expression was somber. "Someone your own age. Someone easy."

Liam sat up. "Don't be an idiot." He grabbed Charlie's shoulders and shook him gently. "You're right. I could have anyone, but you know what? I didn't want anybody. I didn't want to date. I didn't want to do anything but work for a long, long time. And then Portia called, and you needed a ride. And I had to reevaluate what I wanted the moment I set eyes on you." Liam cupped Charlie's jaw and ran a thumb over his lower lip. "And I realized that my daughter is a genius, and that you'd dropped into my life at exactly the perfect moment. So, no more of this self-flagellation nonsense, all right?"

Charlie was already smiling. "No self-flagellation?"

"No." Liam slid his thumb into Charlie's mouth. "No pain. Only pleasure." Charlie bit down on his finger, and Liam's cock stirred again. "Are we done with this conversation?" He moved his hand from Charlie's jaw to the back of his head. "Because there are better ways to pass the time."

"I'm done," Charlie breathed as Liam tightened his fingers in his hair.

"Good." Liam leaned in. "And if ever there comes a time when you want to bring up the whole you're-too-young-for-me thing again, don't."

Charlie laughed. "Okay."

Liam kissed him, not so gently this time. When he ran out of air, he leaned back, and Charlie's expression told him that the man was well and truly finished with all of his self-doubt.

"I'm falling in love with you, you know," Charlie said, voice only slightly uneven.

"I know, love," Liam replied, as he set about making Charlie too breathless to talk at all.

The End

THE FLIGHT

Close Proximity, 4

Erin M. Leaf

Copyright © 2018

Chapter One

Sebastian stared down the length of the swanky private plane, nervous as hell and unable to do a damn thing about it. Plush seats and a polished wooden coffee table stared back mockingly, and he sighed. There was nothing to straighten up or wipe or prep. He'd just have to suck it up and pretend he knew what he was doing. He straightened the cuffs of his shirt for the umpteenth time, wishing he didn't have to wear the dorky sweater on top. It was one of the uglier uniforms he'd had to wear over the years.

"Hey, you okay?" Darlene asked him as she double checked the doors to the galley cabinets. Everything was fastened securely, but Sebastian's friend had always been a bit obsessive-compulsive. He watched her fiddle with the coffeepot before strapping it down.

He nodded and attempted a smile. "I'm fine. Just a little nervous."

"You're going to be fine," Darlene said. "You're a natural with people."

Sebastian's smile turned stiff. "Probably because of all the work I did with my mother."

"Oh, hey." Darlene put a hand on his arm. "I'm sorry. I didn't mean to remind you."

He shook his head. "No, it's fine. It's been over two years since she died. I still miss her, but I don't want to *not* talk about her. I want to remember her, you know?"

Darlene pulled him into a quick hug. "I know. I just didn't mean to remind you." She leaned back and smiled impishly. "Maybe you need to start dating. Maybe this client will be some hot guy and you can practice flirting with him."

"Darlene! You know that's against the rules," Sebastian said, faking shock. He splayed a hand on his chest. "We're not supposed to touch the clients." He huffed. "Besides, I'm not looking for a boyfriend right now. I want to use my free time to focus on my music."

"You're not getting any younger, dude." Darlene laughed. "And rules are meant to be broken."

"I'm only twenty-three," Sebastian said, rolling his eyes. "Give me a break, Darlene."

She smirked at him, and he decided that since he was never going to win an argument with her, he might as well shut up now.

"Heads up," Rob the pilot said, stepping out of the cockpit. "Our passenger is on his way."

Darlene immediately stopped fussing and stood at relaxed attention. After a double-take of his usually relaxed friend, Sebastian did the same as the nerves he'd manage to suppress zipped back up to the surface. He inhaled deeply, and then exhaled, counting to ten. He'd gone through the training, and he knew how to do everything that was expected of him. However, he still wasn't entirely certain what it would be like working for a private charter airline that had wealthy clients. He was used to working on commercial flights filled with beleaguered masses of exhausted travelers.

Can't be worse than cleaning up baby barf and refereeing angry strangers, intent on killing each other, he reminded himself, wishing he was at home working out the kinks in his latest song instead of working. *Gotta pay the rent, though, and music doesn't do that. Yet.*

"There's his car," Darlene said, pointing to a brilliant red Ferrari driving on the tarmac. "It's weird that we don't have a name for the guy, but whatever." She shrugged. "Whatever the client wants, the client gets."

Sebastian shook his head. He couldn't imagine being so rich that you could drive your sports car right up onto the airport and park it next to the plane. A sudden beeping had him turning to the cockpit. The copilot, Phil, pointed to his ear. The pilot frowned, then leaned over and grabbed his headset. He tapped a button and listened for a moment, then murmured a soft "Roger that."

"What is it, Rob?" Darlene asked as he returned.

The pilot sighed. "Your sister is in the hospital, Darlene."

"What?" Darlene's face paled. "Is she all right? What happened?" She scrabbled for her purse in one of the cabinets, and then pulled out her phone. "Come on, come on," she muttered as she waited for it to power up.

Sebastian's heart banged against his ribs. Darlene's younger sister was eighteen, and suffered from seizures.

"They think she's going to be fine, but your mother needs you at the hospital," Rob said, looking grim. "Your sister needs further tests."

"Shit. She's probably going to have to stay overnight, and Mom can't stay with her," Darlene said, already going for her jacket and bag. She glanced at Sebastian. "This is exactly why I pushed you to apply for this job. I need a partner on these transatlantic flights."

Sebastian knew all about Darlene's home life. Her younger sister, Katy, had suffered from epilepsy her entire life, and while it was mostly managed by medication, she couldn't drive and sometimes had difficult episodes. Normally, that wasn't an issue, but Darlene's dad had recently had a stroke, and her mother couldn't take care of both her husband and her daughter by herself.

"Go on. I'll be fine," Sebastian said, projecting a confidence he didn't at all feel.

"You know everyone will understand," Rob said to her.

Darlene sighed as she shoved her arms into her jacket. "I need this job, Rob."

"And you'll keep it." The pilot glanced out of the open hatch. "Go. I'll explain to the client what happened. And then I'll explain it to our boss. Vinair is a good company. They'll be okay with it."

Darlene nodded, then gave Sebastian a quick hug. "Good luck."

"I'll be fine. Give Katy a hug for me." Sebastian returned her hug. "Go on."

She smiled briefly and then ran down the steps. She headed into the terminal just as the doors of the Ferrari opened. Sebastian watched a tall, dark-haired man with large sunglasses get out of the driver's side, while another man exited the passenger's side.

He looks familiar, Sebastian thought, gaze going back to the first man.

"Good. He's on time," Rob murmured from just behind Sebastian.

Sebastian turned to look at the pilot. "Are clients often late?"

The pilot snorted. "You could say that. Rich people aren't like us."

Sebastian grimaced as he watched the two men extract their luggage and head for the plane. "Maybe this guy will be different."

Rob shrugged. "Doesn't matter if he is or isn't."

Yeah, not for you. You're the pilot, and you won't have to interact with him. I will. "I thought there was only one passenger for this flight?" Sebastian asked watching the two men.

"There is. The other guy is his bodyguard," Rob said, as if it were normal for people to have security trailing them around.

And maybe it is, for people like this, Sebastian thought, trying to mentally adjust his thinking. He started down the stairs to help with the luggage. The moment his feet hit the tarmac, he smiled at the two men. "Welcome to Vinair. Let me get your luggage for you, sir." He stared as they walked closer, feeling inexplicably drawn to the man who'd exited the driver's side. The guy wore a blue short-sleeved button-down shirt, thin leather bracelets, and a beautiful silver necklace with a bird charm that nestled in the hollow of his throat. His black jeans were tight, and perfectly paired with a worn pair of shit-kicker boots. He obviously worked out, but he wasn't an over-muscled gym rat.

He looks like an artist, Sebastian thought, itching to find out if the man's blue shirt felt as soft as it looked. He forced his gaze back up to the man's face. He wore his hair relatively short, and had a bit of stubble going on along his jawline. The large mirrored sunglasses hiding his eyes reflected Sebastian's own face back at him with his professional smile firmly pasted on. Sebastian suppressed a grimace. He hated the way the required uniform made him look: conservative and boring. He couldn't even grow his hair out, and usually just opted for a very short cut.

The man smiled. "Thanks," he said, handing his bag to Sebastian.

Huh. He sounds familiar, Sebastian thought as the client turned to the other guy and took the suitcase from him.

"Would you grab my guitar for me, Jack?" The client glanced around. "I don't think anyone is going to jump me right next to the plane, especially after what we had to go through to get the car in here."

The other guy nodded. "No problem, boss." He headed back to the car.

"And stop calling me 'boss'!" sunglasses guy yelled. He grinned when the other man gave him the finger.

Well. He seems nice enough, Sebastian thought, a little less nervous. A guy who would joke like that with his bodyguard couldn't be that much of a dick, no matter how rich he was, right? Still, something about him nagged at Sebastian. The man looked and sounded so damned familiar, but he couldn't put his finger on what it was that twigged his memory.

"Lead the way," sunglasses guy said to Sebastian, jolting him out of his reverie.

Sebastian smiled again, and offered his hand for the other bag. "I can take that for you, sir."

"I've got it." The man lifted the bag with no problem, then stood waiting.

Tearing his gaze away from the man's rock-steady biceps, Sebastian nodded, and then gestured to the stairs. Rob waited at the top for them. "After you, sir," Sebastian said politely. *Best get my mind on my job and not on the client.*

Sunglasses guy lifted an eyebrow. "Are you going to keep calling me 'sir' all the way to Mumbai?" He grinned. "It's a fifteen-hour flight. That's a lot of sirring."

Sebastian swallowed a laugh. "It's my job to sir at you." He waited a beat. "Sir."

The man laughed out loud. "Dear God, no. Please. Just call me Ethan." He turned and headed up the stairs, stepping so lightly his thick boots made no sound.

Wait, what? Ethan? Could it be— Sebastian stared, and then mentally kicked himself into motion. He followed the man up the stairs. There was no way this guy was Ethan Duke Clementine, rock star musician. *No. Way. I'm making wishes out of nothing.* Besides, this guy didn't have long hair. Duke Clementine was known for his long hair and his electric blue eyes.

"He must like you. He's rarely that friendly so fast," a voice said from just behind him.

Sebastian nearly tripped over his own feet. The bodyguard had snuck up on him, carrying a battered guitar case. Plastered across one half were a plethora of stickers from around the world: Milan, New York, Hong Kong, and more. Sebastian blinked. That guitar case had seen a lot of the world. He had a case plastered with stickers just like it at home. "What?"

"Ethan doesn't usually warm up to people that fast," the bodyguard said, following him up the stairs.

We've literally just met. He doesn't know me well enough to like me. Sebastian paused at the entrance to the plane, speculating. *Could he be gay?* He wasn't sure how he felt about flirting with a client, no matter what Darlene said. The pilot had already ducked back into the cockpit, and Ethan was strolling down the length of the plane, bag in hand. "Ethan," he murmured, still trying to figure out where he'd heard that name.

"Yeah. Ethan Clementine," the bodyguard said, propping the guitar against the nearest seat. "Good singer. Nice guy." He clapped a hand against Sebastian's shoulder. "Good luck with him." With that, he turned and exited the plane, making quick work of the stairs and heading for the car, whistling as he walked.

Ethan Clementine. Holy moly, Sebastian thought, shocked into stillness. *I must be dreaming, right?* His thoughts scattered as he stepped back into the plane. There was no way this guy was the same singer whose music he'd been listening to for ten years. Ethan Duke Clementine had burst onto the music scene when Sebastian was thirteen, and he'd been rolling out the hits ever since. He couldn't imagine why the guy would be here, on this particular plane, on this particular day.

Even if it is him, he's at least ten years old than you, and he's straight, so get a grip, Sebastian told himself as he watched Ethan shove his bag into one of the compartments tucked under a side table. If Ethan really *was* Duke Clementine, the musician had cut his hair, and it had rendered him completely unrecognizable. And he was shorter than he looked in interviews, and a hell of a lot thinner. For as long as Sebastian had been aware of Duke as an artist, the man had sported shoulder-length locks. And eyeliner. *You don't know if he's wearing eyeliner or not,* Sebastian mused, still staring. The man had yet to take off his sunglasses.

"You're staring at me," Ethan said, half smiling.

Jesus. That voice... Sebastian flushed. "I'm sorry. Let me get your bag, sir." He forced himself to walk forward. Ethan held out the bag, and Sebastian stowed it in the cabinet near the galley. "You can access it at any time once we're in the air." He turned and grabbed the guitar case. "Did you want to hold onto this? Or I can put it in the closet." He gestured to the rear of the airplane as he stuffed all knowledge of Ethan's probable true identity into a box deep inside his mind. If he didn't, he'd probably start freaking out all over the man, and that would be about as unprofessional as he could get.

Even so, his hands trembled slightly, knowing that he might be holding onto the guitar that had been responsible for the vast majority of his favorite songs. *Maybe it's not really him, and the bodyguard is just playing a joke on me,* he mused, still not letting himself believe Ethan was Duke Clementine, Grammy-winning and bestselling recording artist. *Even my mother liked him, and she wasn't easy to please.* The pang of grief he felt over her death still hurt even though it had been a couple years since she'd passed away. *Even if it is Duke Clementine, keep it together. You've met a ton of musicians over the years, and now is not the time to turn into a fool*, he told himself nervously.

"I've got it. Thanks," Ethan said, smiling again as he strode forward and took the guitar case from Sebastian.

Sebastian nodded and let go, and then turned to take care of the door. The airport ground crew had already started to move the stairs away, and it was a safety violation to keep the door open. When he'd finished sealing it up, he turned to find Ethan looking at him, head tilted.

"Is there something I can help you with?" he asked, pleased that his voice didn't tremble. "Would you like a drink?" He half turned to the galley. "Or I could give you the tour before we take off."

Ethan slowly reached up and removed his sunglasses.

Sebastian froze. The brilliant blue eyes he'd had been half-afraid to see twinkled at him warmly with no sign of any eyeliner anywhere. The thing was, those eyes didn't *need* eyeliner. They were utterly recognizable with or without enhancement, known far and wide all across the world. "No, I'm good," Ethan said, as if from a distance. Sebastian could barely hear the man. He was too busy screaming inside his head. Meanwhile, Ethan's gaze flicked down to Sebastian's nametag. "Sebastian."

Sebastian couldn't move. He couldn't speak. He'd never thought of himself as being particularly shy, but right now, right here, he found himself completely incapable of any response. Ethan, aka Duke Clementine, was standing here, right the hell in front of him, and the man had *said his name.*

Chapter Two

Ethan studied the flight attendant, recognizing the usual signs of a starstruck fan, which was a damned shame. The guy seemed nice before he froze, and Ethan wasn't looking forward to dealing with someone fawning over him for the next fifteen hours or so. *Pity. The man is a looker, too, that's for sure.* Ethan ran his gaze over the guy, taking in the neatly pressed khaki pants and white shirt, and the red uniform sweater the jet company clearly made him wear. The clothes looked like they hid a very fit body. The man's short dark hair and the hint of five-o'clock shadow along his jaw were almost impossibly soft looking. His fingers twitched with the urge to touch before he got hold of himself.

Ethan. Get a grip. No one knows you're bi, and is this really the way you want to come out to the whole world? he asked himself, sighing mentally. "Jack told you who I was, didn't he?" He ran a hand through his hair, wishing that the shorter cut had actually worked to keep his identity a secret for just a bit longer. He hated it when the people he had to interact with treated him like he was some sort of god. He wasn't. He was just a guy who loved making music. *And I'm far from perfect.*

To Ethan's surprise, Sebastian shook off his dazed expression faster than most people. "Um, no. You took off your sunglasses." The man smiled wryly. "You should've worn colored contact lenses or something." He gestured vaguely, then dropped his arm, seeming embarrassed. "Your eyes are really blue, you know."

That surprised a laugh from Ethan. "Huh. You've got a point." He rubbed his jaw, scratching through his short beard. "Maybe I should've dyed my hair, too. Or worn a sack over my head." He eyed the guy through his lashes, wondering if Sebastian swung queer. *Stop it.*

You're not here to seduce the flight attendant, he told himself. His libido thought otherwise, however. His libido liked Sebastian very much, and wasn't at all hesitant in informing Ethan of that fact, evidenced by his cock half-hardening and pressing annoyingly against the zipper of the pants that had seemed comfortable just an hour ago. Now, though, they were irritatingly tight. Ethan resisted the urge to adjust the seam to the left. He refused to get a full-blown erection within minutes of meeting someone. *No,* he told himself firmly. *He's got to be at least ten years younger than you. Maybe more. And you decided you weren't going to do this sort of thing anymore, remember?*

"The haircut is drastic, but it's only going to get you so far." Sebastian waited a beat, and then grinned. "Sir."

Oh, he is gorgeous, Ethan's libido said. Ethan ignored it, telling himself he'd contemplate the mental health ramifications of talking to himself later. "I know, but it was worth a shot," he said out loud, smiling sheepishly. "I was tired of eating my hair."

"I used to have long hair, and I know what you mean," Sebastian said, gesturing to his waist. "Down to here, actually."

Ethan's eyebrows lifted. He couldn't imagine the guy with hair that long, but it seemed a shame that Sebastian now wore it close-cropped. "That's a lot longer than I ever wore mine," he said.

Sebastian shrugged. "I donated it after my mother died."

Ethan frowned. "I'm sorry."

Sebastian shook his head, as if to shrug off Ethan's sympathy. "Anyway, no one is going to bother you on this flight, sir. It's just the two pilots and me. They're going to be busy flying the plane, and I promise to keep my hands to myself." No sooner had the words left the man's mouth when he flushed.

Well, look at that. He really is perfectly gorgeous. Amused and turned on more than he wanted to be, Ethan eased up with the flirting. "I thought I told you to leave off with the sir thing," he said, walking over to one of the plush leather seats. He strapped down his guitar, then looked over the rest of the plane. It wasn't the largest private jet he'd ever flown in, and it wasn't the smallest. *Maybe I should just give in to Barb's nagging and buy one,* he mused, thinking about his manager's latest email. She'd pointed out that it would actually be cheaper to buy, given how often he had to fly.

"It's company policy," Sebastian said. He'd clearly gotten over his embarrassment because he smirked for half a second before pasting another professional smile on his face. "Sir."

Ethan snorted. He could think of any number of other reasons this gorgeous young man would call him "sir", and not one of them had anything to do with being professional. "Why don't you give me the run down on the amenities, Sebastian?" Ethan let the man's name slide out of his mouth like the long note at the end of a song. He might not be able to touch, but he sure as hell could look, right? Sebastian flushed again, but he immediately launched into a well-rehearsed spiel about the plane, the emergency procedures, and where the bathroom was located. Ethan wandered down to the rear of the plane and checked out the toilet and sumptuous bed, not at all surprised by the gleaming fixtures and space. This wasn't his first rodeo, after all. "How soon before takeoff?" he asked, turning back to the main cabin. He trailed his fingers along gleaming wood as he wandered back to the seating area. As if the question was a cue, the pilot came over the speaker to announce imminent departure.

"Momentarily," Sebastian said, eyes twinkling.

Hmpf. He's amused by me. I guess that's better than being starstruck. Ethan sat down and strapped in, then watched Sebastian walk to the front of the plane and sit in the tiny seat provided for flight attendants. "Why don't you come and sit back here? It's only the two of us." He shrugged, ignoring the part of his mind that told him it was his libido talking. He wanted Sebastian close. He shouldn't, but he did.

Sebastian frowned. "I can't, Mr. Clementine. It's—"

Ethan cut him off. "Company policy. I know." He sighed and looked out the window. The tarmac blurred under his gaze from the relentless sun, and he sighed as he tipped his head back and closed his eyes, wishing he weren't going on this trip. Sure, the charity concert was for a good cause, and God knew people in emerging economies like India needed the money for better healthcare, but he was just so freaking tired. Tired of touring. Tired of the whole fame thing. He knew he should be grateful, and he *was,* but being grateful didn't always assuage his exhaustion. *But I'm not tired of the music,* he reminded himself, thinking of his guitar securely strapped down in the next seat over.

"Hey, are you okay?" Sebastian's voice was close, and soft.

Ethan looked over to find the young man had changed seats after all. "I'm fine. Just tired," he said, willing himself not to focus on the guy's full lips. He'd had a number of flings over the years, but none of them had been with men. His last male lover had been a close college friend. He wasn't ashamed of his orientation; he'd just never been in the mood to deal with the fallout to his career. *You're famous enough that you could afford it, now*, a tiny voice prodded him. He ignored it. "I thought you couldn't sit back here with the clients?" he asked, trying to distract himself more than anything else.

Sebastian shrugged. "As long as you don't tell on me." He winked.

Ethan grinned. "Hell, no. I would never out someone." He watched Sebastian flush again, but the man didn't deny anything. *Interesting.* He tilted his head, wanting to set the guy at ease. "It's better than talking to myself. I do that enough already."

Sebastian smiled. "I've heard that's a hallmark of a creative person."

"Or a crazy one," Ethan quipped.

"That too," Sebastian said, brown eyes amused. He glanced at the guitar. "You'll have plenty of time to practice on this flight."

Ethan nodded as the plane began to taxi towards the runway. "True. I'll have to be careful with the humidity levels, or the damn thing will get all out of tune."

"We have a dedicated humidifier for the cabin to help with that," Sebastian said.

"Good." Ethan rested his head against the soft leather. "That's good." He couldn't think of anything else to say. He *wanted* to ask Sebastian if he tasted as good as he looked, but no one said such stupid shit in real life. He closed his eyes, wishing he weren't so fucking lonely. *Poor, little rich man,* he thought, disgusted with himself. He had everything he'd ever wanted, yet here he was, obsessing over the fact that he didn't have anyone to share it with.

"Well. This is awkward," Sebastian said, a hint of amusement in his voice.

Ethan opened his eyes to find the man smiling at him. "What is?"

"I don't want to be that guy, you know, the super

fan who asks you a thousand and one questions,"
Sebastian said, gripping the armrests of the seat as the
plane kicked into takeoff mode. "But I have a thousand
and one questions."

Ethan laughed. "What do you want to know?"
The force of the plane's takeoff pushed him into the
cushions. It was a good thing flying didn't bother him
considering how often he found himself on a plane. "If
you ask me something I don't want to talk about, I'll tell
you. Okay?"

"Deal," Sebastian said. "So, why are you flying to
Mumbai?" He looked around. "And all alone?"

"Those are easy questions. Charity show, and I
wanted some time to myself." Ethan yawned when the
plane leveled off, and then he swallowed and stretched
his jaw. His ears popped. "What about you? What are
you doing here?"

Sebastian raised his eyebrows, then glanced
around the plane. "I work here."

Ethan shook his head. "Yes, but why do this for a
living?"

"The money is pretty good, and I'm not stuck
behind a desk all day." Sebastian looked out the window.
The plane had turned, tipping toward the ground. The
New Jersey coastline stretched into view. "I did
information technology for a while, but I hated crawling
under other people's desks to wiggle loose cables back
where they belonged. So, here I am."

Ethan nodded. "I get that. I was a CPA for a
while, and I did *not* enjoy it."

"Wait, what? You were a CPA, of all things?"
Sebastian's eyebrows rose. "That's not in any of your
interviews."

"I don't like to talk about it because it was a huge
disaster. I was good at the math stuff, but the part where I

had to stare at spreadsheets all day? Not so much." Ethan half smiled. "I have this thing where I can't stand to sit for longer than a couple of hours. I didn't really feel like sharing that with the world. It doesn't paint me in the best light." He lifted a shoulder, still a bit embarrassed, even years later. "I was a terrible CPA." Though, in retrospect, his degree had helped him quite a bit with the financial side of his career, so he didn't totally regret it.

"That's me. That is so totally me. My mother used to tell me I had ants in my pants." Sebastian chuckled, and then unbuckled his seatbelt. He stood up. "Okay, time for drinks. Would you like something to eat? We're supposed to call it dinner, because this is where most people try to get some sleep and get ahead of the jet lag." He smiled wryly. "It's too early to call it dinner, if you ask me."

"Dinner sounds good," Ethan said, amused. Jet lag was a thing he was so used to that he never really managed to get his nights and days on a good schedule. Whatever meal Sebastian wanted to call it was fine with him. Ethan stretched as he watched Sebastian walk away. The man had a tight, perfect ass. *Perfect for kneading.* His cock swelled, and Ethan sighed, frustrated all over again. Sebastian's voice was mellow and warm, and he could easily imagine it as a backing vocal on one of his tracks. "Hmm," he muttered, grabbing his one of his bags from the cabinet under the coffee table where he'd stowed it. He took out a notebook and began jotting down ideas for lyrics. The smell of food broke his concentration a minute later.

"Hey. It's been a couple hours, and I figured you might be hungry by now," Sebastian said, placing a tray on the table.

"Wait, what? A couple hours?" Ethan looked outside, and then checked his watch. "Well. Damn." He hadn't had a good writing session like that in ages. "Looks delicious." He pushed aside his notebook and picked up the sandwich. "Oh, turkey. My favorite."

"That's what it said on the menu that came with your paperwork," Sebastian said, about to walk away.

"Hey, keep me company?" Ethan asked him, looking up with what he hoped was an endearing expression. *I probably just look tired and old.* He smiled, trying to recapture the feeling he'd had while writing. It had felt good. He wanted to feel that way all the time, but he knew it was fleeting.

"You're sure?" Sebastian asked hesitantly.

Ethan nodded emphatically. "Hell, yeah. Believe me, you'll be doing me a favor." He took a bite of the sandwich and moaned. "Jesus. Did you make this? It's delicious. Is that avocado?" He took another bite, then opened his eyes to find Sebastian staring at his mouth. *This dude is definitely gay*, Ethan thought, keeping his smirk to himself with some effort.

"Uh, yeah, I made it," Sebastian said. "I read somewhere that you like avocado so I took a few liberties with the menu." The man jiggled his leg, looking uncomfortable. "Sorry. I know it's odd that I know that."

Ethan shrugged. "Strangers know all sorts of random things about me."

Sebastian grimaced. "Fame is weird."

"True story," Ethan said emphatically.

Sebastian ducked his head down. "This is awkward. Usually when you meet someone, small talk is easy, but I already know about—"

Ethan cut the poor guy off before he strangled himself with embarrassment. "Hey. It's okay. I get it." He grabbed the glass of water Sebastian had brought with the sandwich and chugged half of it down. "My life has basically been an open book for a decade."

"Not everything. I had no idea that you'd worked as a CPA," Sebastian countered, leaning back in the seat.

Ethan preferred him that way: relaxed and smiling. "But you already knew I had a degree in finance, right? I never tried to hide that."

Sebastian flushed. "Well, yeah."

Ethan shrugged. "That's my life. I knew going into this business that if I hit it big I would have to take the good with the bad. The lack of privacy is part of the deal."

"Is that why you don't drink?" Sebastian frowned. "Most people have already polished off a bunch of cocktails by now on a flight this long."

"I never wanted booze to define me, so I made the choice to avoid it." Ethan chuckled. "I'm not much of a rock star, am I? I don't drink, I don't smoke…" He shrugged. "Alcohol and smoke fuck up my voice." Ethan finished off the sandwich and drank the rest of the water. "I'm a little insane about keeping my vocal cords healthy, you know?"

"That's sensible. Your voice is your career." Sebastian sat up. "I never read that anywhere."

"That's because I never told anyone. It's not a big deal. It's just part of my life, like brushing my teeth." Ethan grabbed his notebook again, then frowned down at it and set it aside. He needed the guitar for the next part.

"Am I bothering you?" Sebastian stood up.

"No, no. Sit down," Ethan said as Sebastian grabbed the tray. He mock scowled until Sebastian capitulated. "I want you to listen to something."

Sebastian's eyebrows rose. "Me?"

Ethan nodded. "Yeah. I need some fresh ears."

"Wow." Sebastian stared at him, and then cleared his throat. "Okay, give me a second to stow this first, okay?"

Ethan waved at him, already reaching for his guitar. He had an idea he needed to play with, and he didn't want to lose it. There was something about Sebastian's voice that drew it out. He opened the case and pulled out his precious Martin acoustic, and then strummed a few chords. It wasn't the most expensive instrument he owned, but it was his first good one, and he'd carted it around the world for years. "Hmm. Maybe an A," he murmured, trying another riff.

"Sounds nice."

Ethan glanced up. "It's just a chord. But I have something in mind." He started playing a few notes, watching Sebastian's face as he worked, and when the man's expression suddenly relaxed, he knew he had the progression he wanted. "Ha. That's it," he said, humming lightly. If he could just get it to work right…

"Try a minor beneath the chord. The harmonics are there. You just have to…" Sebastian trailed off when Ethan looked up at him. "What?"

Ethan blinked, then laughed. "You're right." He tried what Sebastian suggested, and it worked beautifully. "Do you play?"

Sebastian shrugged. "My mom was into music. I play a few instruments."

Ethan nodded. He tried a few more riffs, then settled on a simple melody to lay on top of the whole thing. Sebastian chimed in a few more times, and then he started humming. Ethan almost dropped his guitar when he heard the man's husky, warm voice sliding in between the notes. His cock hardened painfully, but he didn't want to lose the thread of creativity so he tried to ignore his raging lust. It wasn't easy. Sebastian kept singing, driving him crazy. Ethan played another measure. They worked back and forth for a few hours, until the song and part of another was on the page, and Ethan had a serious case of blue balls. He shifted his weight, trying to give his cock more room, but it didn't help.

"Hmm. I like it," Sebastian said, smiling and sitting back. Given the coy glances Sebastian had been giving Ethan the entire time, Ethan knew the man had noticed his hard-on. And he hadn't objected. "And it's time to get some sleep. We've been at it for almost five hours," Sebastian continued.

This guy is fucking brilliant, and I want to screw him into the floor, Ethan thought, afraid to question this gift that had suddenly dropped into his lap out of nowhere. He'd never been able to work easily with others when writing music, but collaboration was the name of the game. *But this was so easy. What the hell is this guy doing stuck on an airplane?* His thoughts trailed off as Sebastian hummed another variation to the bridge. *This man is perfect.* Heat and need dueled for position in his body, and it was all he could do to keep his hands to himself.

"Sebastian," he said finally, laying his fingers on the strings. He was so fucking turned on his voice had gone hoarse. "I don't want to sleep."

"Wait a second, Ethan. That last part, here…" Sebastian tilted his head, clearly lost in thought again. Finally, he pointed to the sprawl of notes they'd scribbled on the paper over the last hour or so. "This part. Try it with a different chord. I think you almost had it."

When Ethan didn't reply, Sebastian looked up, and then flushed. "Oh." Ethan didn't know what the guy saw on his face, but it must have been something intense, because Sebastian bit his lip and went still. He looked like a kid who'd just been caught with his hand in the cookie jar. "Shit, I'm sorry, man." He tried to stand up, but Ethan grabbed his forearm, leaving Sebastian half-standing, arm awkwardly askew in front of him.

"Please. Don't go." Ethan tugged him down, and Sebastian tentatively perched on the edge of the seat. "I've never been able to work with anyone like this before."

"Wait. What?" Sebastian stared at him. "Never? But you collaborate all the time." He tugged at the sleeves of his ugly sweater as if it were big enough to hide him from Ethan's view. "And I have to get the cabin ready so you can sleep."

"I don't want to sleep. And yes, I collaborate sometimes, but I hate every minute of it," Ethan said, startling himself with the truth of it. "Every time I have to work with someone else, it takes twice as long to write a song, and it drives me crazy, but I have to do it. That's how the business works."

"I'm sorry," Sebastian said again after a long pause, but Ethan was already shaking his head.

"No. Don't apologize. Working with you here, well…" Ethan trailed off, not knowing how to say what he felt, probably because he was so fucking confused he couldn't figure it out himself. He ignored the voice inside his head that told him he was aroused, not confused. The last thing he wanted to do was start something he couldn't finish.

Sebastian tilted his head. "You're not at all what I expected."

Ethan frowned. "What did you expect?"

Sebastian flushed again, and then he glanced down at their notes. He didn't speak.

Ethan reached over, then stopped halfway. When Sebastian looked up, electricity danced down Ethan's spine. Sebastian's brown eyes had darkened to black, and Ethan knew that the man in front of him knew exactly what he wanted, but he didn't know if he could have it. Ethan bit his lip, hard. His attraction to Sebastian was intense and unexpected, and he wanted to give Sebastian what he wanted. *No, be honest, Ethan,* he told himself. *You want it, too.*

"Don't play with me, Ethan," Sebastian said, voice low.

As if in a dream, Ethan moved his hand forward. The moment it touched Sebastian's shoulder, he knew that nothing would be the same ever again.

Chapter Three

The moment Ethan's fingers touched his shoulder, Sebastian wrapped his fingers around the musician's wrist and drew him closer. He had no idea if the man was into guys, but he didn't particularly care at this point. He'd given the rock star an out, and Ethan hadn't pulled away. "I know we've just met—" he murmured, but Ethan slid his hand up and put a finger on his lips. Sebastian shuddered. He'd been in a constantly shifting state of embarrassment, nervousness, and arousal from the moment Ethan had stepped onto the plane, and this sure as hell wasn't helping restore his equanimity.

"I told myself I wasn't going to do this anymore," Ethan said cryptically, and then he leaned in.

"Do what?" Sebastian tried to ask, but Ethan's mouth met his and all hell broke loose in his body. He groaned, arms going for Ethan's hair, but the musician knocked his hands away and climbed up onto his lap. Sebastian froze, then swallowed hard when his cock pressed up into the juncture of Ethan's legs.

"Fuck, you're gorgeous," Ethan muttered, and then he kissed Sebastian again.

Sebastian gripped Ethan's ass through the soft jeans, mind whirling. Ethan tasted like insanity and heat, and he couldn't get enough. When Ethan finally lifted his head, Sebastian gasped, barely able to catch his breath. His cock was so fucking hard he was afraid he would go off in his pants. His lips stung. "You're into guys?" he asked, and then he bit his lower lip in frustration. What a stupid question. The man was on his *lap,* for God's sake. *Duke Clementine just kissed me,* he thought inanely, and then he wondered if he was dreaming, but the weight of the man on his legs felt all too real.

Ethan laughed. "Yeah. I'm into guys. I'm bi, not

that I advertise it. I don't need the hassle." He rolled his hips, pushing his erection into Sebastian's abdomen. "I'm assuming you're into guys, too, or you would've dumped me on my ass, right?"

"Uh," Sebastian said, not really able to think clearly. *Dump the hottest man I've ever seen onto the floor? Yeah, no.* Ethan rolled his hips again. "Oh my God," Sebastian said, gritting his teeth. He *would not* come in his pants like a damned teenager. "Fuck." He banged his head against the soft cushions of the seat even as his hands kneaded Ethan's ass. He wanted to suck Ethan off. He wanted to fuck him. He wanted all sorts of things he hadn't thought about wanting in far too long.

"Relax, Sebastian," Ethan said, cupping his face. "I'm not going anywhere."

Sebastian laughed, then moaned when Ethan leaned in closer. "I feel like I'm dreaming," Sebastian said.

"Don't think so hard," Ethan replied, kissing him again and again, until Sebastian stopped trying to figure out why Duke Clementine chose him, of all people, to do this with. There had been literally no hint of Ethan being bisexual anywhere in the media, so for him to do this now, and with *Sebastian,* shocked the hell out of him.

"You know I won't tell anyone," Sebastian gasped out.

Ethan stilled. "I know," he said, and then he started to unbutton his shirt.

Sebastian stared as the man's lean torso slowly came into view. Ethan had a collection of tattoos scattered across his body, and though nothing Sebastian saw was new to him—the musician had done a number of interviews with photos of his body spread in glossy high definition across numerous platforms—there was something entirely shocking about being able to touch instead of just look. "Seeing you in a magazine is nothing like being here in real life," he murmured, reaching up to trace a finger across warm skin.

"This is real life, Sebastian," Ethan said, voice warm and husky. He sucked in a breath when Sebastian's fingers trailed down the middle of his chest to the waistband of his jeans and back up again.

"I want to suck you off," Sebastian said, trying to make himself move, but his fingers were too busy learning every last inch of ink on Ethan's skin.

"What a good idea," Ethan said, standing up, but instead of undoing his jeans, he went to his knees.

"What are you doing?" Sebastian asked, sitting up. He tried to drag Ethan back to his feet, but the rock star put his hands on Sebastian's pants and undid the zipper. He slid his fingers inside. Sebastian gasped when those fingers brushed against his cock.

"This is the ugliest uniform I've ever seen," Ethan said, fingers drawing down Sebastian's underwear. He licked his lips as Sebastian's erection sprang out.

Sebastian's hips bucked. "Oh, God." Ethan's electric blue eyes stared up at him. "You're killing me, Ethan."

"No, I can't do this while you're wearing that hideous sweater," Ethan said unexpectedly, reaching for Sebastian's top. He tugged on it. "Take it off."

Sebastian nearly tore it in his hurry to get it off his body. "This is crazy."

Ethan undid the buttons of Sebastian's shirt, and then he reached down and gripped his cock in a firm, warm hand. "Yeah, it's crazy, but I'm not sure I care." He leaned in and sucked Sebastian's erection into his mouth.

Sebastian jammed the heel of his hand against his mouth, hips jerking. He didn't want to thrust. He didn't want to do anything that would hurt Ethan. *Shit, maybe this isn't a good idea. What if I push into his throat? He needs to be able to sing. He said he's paranoid about his vocal cords.* He reached down and pulled Ethan up.

"What?" Ethan licked down the side of Sebastian's erection.

"I don't want to hurt you. You need to sing tomorrow," Sebastian said, barely able to put the words together.

Ethan laughed. "You're worried about my voice?"

Sebastian flushed.

"Giving head is not going to wreck my vocal cords," Ethan said, sounding amused. "But there are other things we can do, if you prefer." He stood up.

Sebastian stared as Ethan stripped off the rest of his clothes. He looked strong and sure of himself, and Sebastian's mind flashed on one of the interviews he remembered reading. They'd been talking to some of the fans at one of Ethan's concerts, and a girl they'd interviewed had said that Duke Clementine was pure sex when he was on stage. *If Ethan is pure sex on stage, off stage he's lethal,* Sebastian thought, digging his fingers into the cushions. He couldn't believe he was actually doing this. "You realize this is insane."

Ethan leaned over and carefully moved his guitar to the seat behind him, brushing his fingers over the strings as he let go. The sound of a chord lingered in the air, quietly tantalizing. "Maybe it is," he murmured, and then he straightened up. His blue eyes had darkened with arousal. Sebastian couldn't look away. Ethan's cock was thick and hard, and Sebastian wanted it inside him in the worst way. He swallowed thickly as Ethan went to his knees. His hands went to Sebastian's pants and wrestled them off. "Take off your shirt," he said.

Sebastian obeyed, half crazed with lust. "I'm going to get fired for this."

Ethan shook his head. "No one will know." He climbed back onto the sofa, legs going on either side of Sebastian's hips. "No one ever has to know."

Sebastian hissed out a breath when Ethan's smooth skin slid along his. He wasn't sure how he felt about being Ethan's little secret, but he also didn't want to stop. *I can have this. It doesn't have to mean anything,* he told himself, knowing that even as he thought the words they were wrong. It *did* matter. He *did* care. *But even if Ethan vanishes after this, I'm doing it anyway.*

"God, look at you. Who knew you were hiding this gorgeousness under that hideous uniform," Ethan said, running his hands down Sebastian's chest. "You're built like a thoroughbred."

Sebastian flushed, but couldn't get his voice to work. Instead of answering, he gripped Ethan's arms and thrust up. "Ethan," he gasped, hips moving. Their cocks slid together, and it was both too much and not enough sensation all at once.

"Can I fuck you?" Ethan asked suddenly.

Sebastian groaned as his skin prickled from head to toe. Like he was going to say *no* to *that*? "Yeah. Of course." It had been a good while since he'd bottomed, but there was no way he'd pass this up. Not now, when they were both naked and desperate. "Lube and condoms are in the cabinet." He pointed behind him.

Ethan leaned his forehead on Sebastian's and breathed deep for a moment, as if struggling for control, and then he grinned. "You stock condoms and lube?"

"Standard supplies," Sebastian managed to say, even as he wanted to grip Ethan hard and fuck up into his warm body. He inhaled, forcing his thoughts into some semblance of order. "We always stock lube and condoms." The clients on these planes wanted their fun, and they wanted their privacy. "No cameras, either, so we can do whatever," he mentioned, knowing that the pilot couldn't peek in on them.

"Good. That's good." Ethan kissed him, quick and hard. "Don't move." He got up and headed for the cabinet.

Sebastian watched him walk, mouth watering at the muscles that slid beneath the ink on his skin. Ethan was a hell of a man. A hell of a musician. He gripped his cock and squeezed, hoping the pressure would keep him from going off the moment Ethan returned. "You realize we only met a few hours ago," he found himself saying.

Ethan walked back over and tossed supplies on top of the notebook on the coffee table. "I know. And I don't do this. I haven't hooked up with someone like this in years." He sat down. "Come here." Sebastian leaned up, and Ethan kissed him again, grabbing his ass. "Do you want to stop? I understand if you do."

Sebastian thought about it for a half-second, and then he shook his head. To hell with the consequences. So what if he got hurt? He'd been hurt before. *And I like Ethan. I like the guy behind the Duke Clementine persona, which is just astonishing.* His thoughts scattered when he looked at Ethan's cock again. "Hell, no," he said aloud. He didn't want any misunderstandings.

"Thank God." Ethan grinned, and then his hand was on Sebastian's erection. "Let me in, Sebastian." He rubbed his thumb over the tip, making Sebastian shudder. "Let me in. I promise I won't hurt you."

That's a promise you can't keep, Sebastian thought, but he didn't care. He opened his legs and closed his eyes as Ethan reached for the lube. He felt as if he was going to vibrate out of his skin if Ethan didn't hurry up. "Come on, Ethan," he said, squirming when the man's slick fingertip teased at his hole. "I can take it."

"I know you can take it, but I want more than that. I want you to enjoy it," Ethan said, adding another finger. He teased and rubbed until Sebastian's muscles eased. "I want you to forget where we are. I want you to forget your name." He slid a third finger inside, and Sebastian moaned, hips jerking. "That's it," Ethan muttered, hitting the spot inside that drove Sebastian crazy.

"Fuck," he said, voice ragged. "Ethan."

"Yeah, I've got you," Ethan said, still torturing him with his fingers. Sebastian's cock was hard as steel and desperate for attention. He tried to grab himself, but Ethan stopped him.

"Not yet."

"Fuck, you're killing me," Sebastian said, clenching his muscles around the fingers slowly driving him out of his fucking mind. "I'm ready. I'm beyond ready."

Ethan kissed him, and removed his fingers. "All right." He leaned back, grabbing a condom.

Sebastian watched him rip it open and roll it down his erection. "I hope you know I'm not fragile."

Ethan paused for a moment, blue eyes glittering with a thousand and one unspoken thoughts. Gone was the rock star mystique, and all that was left was a man who looked a little bit tired and a whole lot beautiful. Sebastian caught his breath. *I could fall in love with this man,* he realized, thinking of how good it had felt to write music together. *Fuck.*

"But maybe *I* am," Ethan murmured. Before Sebastian could respond, Ethan eased his legs apart and pushed the head of his cock inside. They both shuddered, and Ethan stilled, dropping his head on Sebastian's shoulder.

"Don't stop now," Sebastian said raggedly. "God, Ethan—" He broke off, trying to breathe. Trying to keep to himself the words that wanted to spill out. Now wasn't the time to tell Ethan how much he wanted *more*. Hell, there might never be time for that.

"Yeah. Yeah, I know," Ethan said, teeth gritted. He gripped Sebastian's shoulders, and then he worked himself the rest of the way inside. "God. You're so fucking hot."

Sebastian groaned, digging fingertips into Ethan's skin. "You're so fucking hard." He squirmed, trying to get the man to move. "Come on. Move."

Ethan hissed out a breath, and then he began to fuck Sebastian in earnest. Sebastian hung onto him for dear life, loving the way Ethan's expression opened up the closer he got to the edge. "Come on, Ethan. Give it up."

Ethan shook his head. "Too soon."

Sebastian huffed out a breath, then reached down to stroke himself. Ethan batted his hand away and took over. The callouses on his fingertips scraped the sensitive skin of Sebastian's erection in precisely the right way. He moaned, spine bowing as his climax rushed through him, despite trying to hold it back.

"Oh, fuck," Ethan hissed. "I can feel you coming around me." He fucked harder, ramming into Sebastian's prostate with uncanny precision and drawing out the pleasure until Sebastian thought he might lose his mind. He shivered as another wave rocked through him, and then Ethan tensed up, shuddering. Sebastian reached up and grabbed Ethan's face, kissing him until the rock star moaned and slumped on top of him, shaking and panting.

"Fucking hell," Ethan muttered, a long time later.

Sebastian snorted. He felt pretty damned wrecked himself. "Yeah. What you said."

"We're going to hell," Ethan said. He heaved himself up, and disposed of the condom before slumping back down against Sebastian.

Sebastian grinned. "I know this might be your first stroll down the rainbow trail in a long time, but gay sex is not an automatic entry into Eviltown, dude."

Ethan laughed. "I know. It's just that we destroyed the sofa."

Sebastian looked down. Lube and jizz streaked the soft leather. "It wipes clean. And even if it didn't, it would just be replaced. You bought the premium service when you booked this flight, Ethan."

Ethan snorted. "My assistant booked the flight." He stroked a hand down Sebastian's arm. "And this isn't my first time with a guy. It's just..." His voice trailed off. "It's been a while."

"Hey." Sebastian went up on an elbow, ignoring the slight ache in his ass. He'd pay for the sex later, but it didn't matter now. "Are you okay?" He touched Ethan's hip. He'd wanted to cuddle and ride out the afterglow, but it was clear his lover didn't feel the same way.

Ethan grimaced. "I'm an idiot."

Oh no. Please no homophobic freakout. I know he said he was bi, but still. Sebastian frowned. "What are you so worried about? I already said I'd never tell anyone." And he wouldn't. He didn't want anyone else to know how hard and fast he'd fallen. *Because it's a total cliché to fall in love with a rock star.*

Ethan shook his head. He should've looked absurd, lounging naked on the sofa with his hair a mess, but he didn't. He looked like sex and lightning, with his blue eyes and smooth skin and colorful tattoos. And for a single, perfect second, Sebastian experienced the most astonishing moment of clarity: Duke Clementine was nothing but smoke and mirrors, and Ethan was the real truth, not that it mattered.

My heart is already halfway broken, Sebastian mused. This man who'd just fucked him into oblivion had just blown Sebastian's world into tiny bits and remade it into something else entirely. Ethan had edged everything with just a bit of the sparkle that Sebastian would never be able to hold again. He inhaled slowly, not wanting to chase this feeling away, but of course, nothing so brilliant could last. He blinked, and Ethan was still looking at him, soft and tired and gorgeous. "Ethan?"

Ethan sighed and ran a hand through his hair. "I really fucking like you, Sebastian."

Join the club. Sebastian frowned. "And this is a problem, uh, why?"

"Because I'm going to be gone in approximately—" He looked at his watch. "Six hours. And after that, I'm going out on tour for months." He looked back up at Sebastian. His blue eyes were shadowed. "I don't want to be that guy. That famous guy." He snorted. "Love them and leave them, you know? That's why I stopped doing this sort of thing."

Sebastian chewed on his lip for a moment. "I knew the deal, Ethan. I said yes, remember?" He'd known it before the first kiss, when they were in the middle of writing a song together. He was just a lowly flight attendant, trying to scrape together enough money to pay off the loans he'd needed to take care of his mother while she was dying. And Ethan was, well... Ethan was Duke Clementine. Famous musician. The unattainable man everyone wanted, but no one got to keep.

Ethan grimaced. "*You* might have known the deal, but I don't think I did." He sighed and let his head fall back onto the sofa.

Sebastian leaned into him. He swallowed the lump in his throat, which was ridiculous. No one fell in love after just a few short hours. "No one was hurt here, Ethan. Let it go," he finally said. "It's okay."

Ethan sighed, and kissed Sebastian.

Sebastian kissed him back. He didn't have any other words to offer.

Chapter Four

Hours later, Ethan woke up with a mouth on his cock, and the scent of lemon tea in the air.

"Nothing else was waking you up," Sebastian said, and then he bent his head down again, licking leisurely up the length of Ethan's erection.

Ethan groaned, hips thrusting. "What the fuck? Sebastian?"

Sebastian smirked, dark eyes bright with lust. "Not fucking. Giving head, Ethan. Get with the program." He cupped Ethan's balls, then sucked his cock back inside a mouth that was too damned hot to be entirely real. "God."

Ethan threw his head back, thinking of the music they'd made earlier. It was the most honest stuff he'd written in years, and here was Sebastian, sucking his cock with filthy abandon. He shuddered, and Sebastian bit down gently on the head of his shaft, driving him mad with need. "Oh fuck," he gasped, writhing. He fisted his hands in the sheets, grateful that this plane had a bed.

"Let go, Ethan," Sebastian said, and then he sucked harder.

Ethan didn't have any damned choice but to let go. He was too close to the edge for anything else. He let out another moan, and then the next thing he knew, he was bucking up into that perfect mouth as his cock jerked. Pleasure rushed through him like the top of a mountain exploding. His entire body spasmed, and then he collapsed, panting, as he tried to figure out what had just happened. His feet were tangled in a soft blanket, and his head spun. "Fuck, Sebastian. Come here."

He tried to drag Sebastian up and over him, but the man instead knelt up on the mattress, stroking himself fast and hard as he stared at Ethan with dark eyes. He'd put his shirt on, unbuttoned, but nothing else. He looked like sex and home. Ethan's heart lurched. "Sebastian, let me—"

"Too late," Sebastian interrupted, and then he climaxed. His fingers tightened around his erection as he bowed over. Jets of semen landed on Ethan's chest. He licked his lips as he saw the wild look on Sebastian's face. "Oh, shit. I'm sorry," Sebastian wheezed, hand still gripping his cock like a man about to go over a cliff. "Didn't mean to make a mess."

He's worried about making a mess? Ethan couldn't even wrap his brain around that. It was his head and his heart that were a mess, not his body. "Hey. No apologies."

Sebastian tried to wipe at him with a tissue, and Ethan grabbed his wrist. "It's fine," he said, even while he knew it was absolutely *not* fine. Nothing about this insanity was fine. What the hell did he think he was doing, fooling around with this guy? Hadn't he told himself he wasn't going to do this anymore?

You've never done this, a voice in his head said, and Ethan knew it was the truth, even as he ignored it. Sebastian wasn't anything like the random flings he used to have when he was a thousand years younger and ten million times less jaded. He glanced at the windows, but the shades were drawn. He had no idea how many hours had passed since he'd fallen asleep, or how close they were to landing, but he had a feeling that he had no time left with Sebastian. A pang of anxiety hit him, and he reached out. "Come here." He dragged the younger man down on top of him, ignoring the mess on his chest. "Jesus. What a way to wake up."

"Well, I made you some tea, thinking the caffeine would help you wake up, but you were *out,* man," Sebastian mumbled. "And we're landing in a half hour.

You must have been exhausted."

Ethan's heart rate sped up. "Shit. Yeah. I don't sleep well, usually." He stroked his hands over Sebastian's hair. The guy wore it short, and something about running his fingers through the soft ends soothed Ethan. "I wish we had more time."

Sebastian lifted his head. "Do me a favor?"

"Anything," Ethan promised.

"Finish that second song we started, okay?"

Of all the things Sebastian could have asked for, that one wasn't what Ethan had expected. "Of course," he said. As if he would ignore the most real and honest piece of music he'd created in forever. "Hey, what's your last name?"

Sebastian frowned, sitting up to run his hand over his face. "My last name?"

Ethan nodded. "I need it to give you songwriting credit."

Sebastian blinked. He looked surprised, and that thought hurt Ethan. Did the guy think he'd *steal* his work?

"My last name is Hunter," he said slowly, as if he really didn't want Ethan to know it, which was just weird. He looked around, and then he grabbed his pants and yanked them on. "Dammit. I need to get myself together. There's no *time,*" Sebastian muttered.

"Hmm. Hunter. Sounds familiar," Ethan said, reaching for his notebook. He scribbled "Sebastian Hunter" on the last page of the first song they'd written together, and then he looked up. Sebastian had already managed to put himself together, mostly. The beard burn on his jawline was a dead giveaway, but Ethan couldn't bring himself to point it out. He suppressed the urge to ask for a picture. He didn't want any reminders of how much he liked this man. *And, too, it's usually the fans who ask* me *for pictures, not the other way around,* he thought sardonically.

"You should get dressed," Sebastian said, handing over Ethan's clothes. He'd folded them.

Ethan shook his head. "Yeah. I know." He stared up at the handsome, young, completely unattainable flight attendant. He would *not* upend this man's life. He couldn't. Sebastian didn't deserve it. And that's why Ethan had spent the last ten years alone. No one should have to put up with his schedule, and the crazed fans, and the traveling. "You'll take care of yourself?" he asked like an idiot, instead of saying what he *should* be saying, which was "forget me". Or maybe, "please stay". He looked down, ashamed to even consider it.

Sebastian's expression tightened. "Of course. I'm a grown man, Ethan. And I've been taking care of myself for a long time."

Ethan shook his head. He wanted to ask for Sebastian's number. He could promise to call him. "Okay," he said, instead. Doing the right thing sucked. Or maybe it was the wrong thing—he couldn't tell anymore.

Sebastian nodded, eyes dark. His expression had faded into neutral. "Okay."

****

Three months later, Ethan stared at the wall of his dressing room, exhausted and numb. He'd just finished another wildly successful show, in yet another city, and he felt like complete and utter shit.

"Duke! The fans are waiting," his manager and assistant, Barb, said, barging in without so much as a knock. "Pick yourself up, man." She frowned at him and grabbed his leather jacket and a bottle of water. "Here, drink this. You're probably dehydrated."

"My name is Ethan," he said stubbornly. He

didn't have the energy for anything *but* stubborn anymore. Stubborn was what got him up on stage. Stubborn was what kept him from snapping the head off of anyone who tried to ask him how he was doing. He was doing just fine, thank you. *Except I'm totally not.*

"Ethan." She sighed and thrust the bottle under his nose. "Drink."

He cracked it open and swallowed half of it. She was right. He *was* thirsty. "I can't do this anymore," he said suddenly, wiping his face with the towel she held out. He hadn't known those words were going to come out of him until they were already hanging in the air. Barb's shocked expression told him everything he needed to know.

"You can't do what? Perform?" She glanced around the room, looking for drugs or porn or who the hell knew. He hadn't indulged in that shit in years.

"I can't do this tour. Sing. Be Duke Clementine," he said, shrugging on his jacket. It hid his tattoos, but more importantly, it hid the weight he'd lost since the Mumbai charity concert. "I want to be Ethan."

"What the hell are you talking about? You *are* Ethan. And you've got four more months of this tour, with sold out shows, might I remind you. And a number one album. Your music is selling like hotcakes." She glared at him. "Have you lost your mind?"

Ethan grimaced. He knew she didn't mean to sound so abrasive, but his words had come at her out of left field. "Maybe." He sat back down and leaned his head against the sofa. The trays of food and booze and all the other things the venue had set up for him didn't interest him. Hanging out with the band after the concert, something he used to love doing, didn't interest him. Even meeting the fans, which was a highlight of touring, didn't interest him. An image of Sebastian smiling drifted through his head and he scowled. *No. You can't have him,* he told himself.

She stared at him for a moment, and then her expression softened as she sat down next to him. "Hey, Ethan."

He looked at her.

"You realize that you've been performing with more heart lately than I've ever heard from you? Everyone's noticed. That's why your music is hitting all the charts," she said quietly. "It's like you've suddenly got something big inside you, and you're holding onto it really tight, and you only let it out when you perform."

Ethan shook his head. "I have no idea what you're talking about."

She pursed her lips. "What's his name?"

Ethan sat straight up. "What?" Barb didn't know about Sebastian. How the hell could she? They'd been alone on that plane, except for the two pilots. He'd set it up that way deliberately, so he could get some rest from the whole entourage thing. *I got a hell of a lot more than rest, though.* Sebastian hadn't come out of the plane once it'd landed, and Ethan knew why. He hadn't wanted to watch him go, and he didn't blame the guy.

"I know you met someone, Ethan, come on. I've known you for ten years, remember? I was your friend before I was your manager." She took the bottle of water from him and set it aside. "Who is he?"

"Why do you assume it's a he?" he retorted, then winced. He'd as much as just admitted he'd met someone.

She rolled her eyes. "You may be bi, and I know you appreciate women, but your emotions are solidly gay, my friend."

Ethan stared at her. "That's not a thing."

"It totally is a thing," she retorted immediately.

"Some people fall in love with women, and some people fall in love with men. I've known you swung both ways for a while now, but you've never fallen in love." She stood up. "Until now. So, spill it. What's his name?"

Ethan's heart started pounding. Should he tell her? "I only knew him for a few hours. It's not love."

"I met my boyfriend one night and a day later we were shacked up together, so don't give me that bullshit." She snapped her fingers under his nose. "His name, Ethan. I can't help you if I don't know who he is."

"What? So you can go upend his life?" He rubbed his face, probably smearing his eyeliner. "My life is a nightmare of touring and paparazzi. No one deserves that, Barb."

"You don't know unless you ask. Maybe he'd be cool with that kind of lifestyle," she said. "You're making decisions for him, and I think it's because you're afraid of what he might say."

Ethan exhaled, frustrated.

"You know I'm just going to keep asking you. You might as well tell me who he is now, and save us both the trouble." Barb lifted an eyebrow.

He rolled his eyes. "You can be such a nag."

"If it works." Barb tucked her straight blonde hair behind an ear. "Give me his name."

"Fine, whatever," Ethan growled. "His name is Sebastian Hunter. He was the flight attendant on the plane I took to Mumbai for that charity thing." Barb was like a dog with a bone when she wanted something. Of course, that's what made her a fantastic manager and an even better friend. "Happy, now?"

She nodded, tapping into her phone. "Hunter. Got it. Does he know music?"

"Actually, yeah." Ethan frowned. "We wrote a song, and part of another one together on the plane. I was in a bad place that day. He really helped when I pulled out my guitar." He shook his head, still mystified by that transcendent session. "It was weird. He really knew his stuff, yet he said he didn't work in the industry." He lifted a shoulder. "He seemed sad. Said his mom had died two years ago."

"Wait a second," Barb said. She chewed on the inside of her cheek for a moment. "He could be Sue Hunter's son. I heard he had a ton of loans to pay back for her care after her damned manager took off with all of her money, the bastard. I can't remember her son's name, but I can look it up."

"Wait. What? Sue Hunter? The songwriter?" Ethan asked, confused. Her music had been in demand by all kinds of artists—country, folk, pop. She'd written a lot of hits for other singers in the past twenty years. "Are you serious? What are the odds that her kid would be working on my flight?"

"Sue Hunter died from complications after she had surgery for pancreatic cancer. Her son took care of her. He was just barely legal at the time, but everyone knew how good a musician he was because he used to help her with her work. The kid was a fucking prodigy. But after she died, he fell off the radar," Barb said, frowning. "Word is they had no money, because her manager owned all the stuff she'd done over the years. It was a hell of a thing."

That's awful, Ethan thought, once again grateful for his degree. He'd never had that kind of trouble. He shook his head. "That's insane. Why would he be working as a flight attendant?"

She shrugged. "Who knows? Maybe because no one would hire him? He never got any credit for his work with his mother, but I know he had skills. His mother and I crossed paths a couple times before I started working with you exclusively."

"What the fuck," Ethan muttered, rubbing his eyes. *Sebastian Hunter. A prodigy.* He'd never worked with anyone that easily, ever. That had to be why Sebastian was so damned good at songwriting. It hadn't even occurred to him to ask his background. "I have a couple songs that we wrote on the plane, Barb. They're brilliant. I haven't played them for anyone yet." *Because I'm a fucking idiot.*

"New songs? And Sebastian Hunter helped write them?" Barb's eyes gleamed. "I want to hear them."

"What? Now?"

"Yes," she said, expression eager. "Right the hell now, Ethan."

Ethan frowned, but the look on her face told him he wasn't going to get out of this. "Jesus, Barb. Fine." He grabbed his guitar, and played the opening chord of the first song. He had no need to get his notebook. He didn't need to practice. He knew both songs by heart. He looked at his manager, almost daring her to say a word, and then he started singing. After the last notes faded, he swallowed hard, and put the guitar back in the case. His emotions were all over the damn place. "We started working on another one. I finished it a few days ago." He didn't tell her that the second song was a love song, and that he'd written it for Sebastian. From her expression, she already knew.

"Jesus Christ, Ethan," Barb said, wiping the tears off her face. "We need to record that, pronto. And maybe the second one, too, if it's just as good."

"The first song is sad. It makes sense, now that I know about Sebastian's mom. We were both really messed up that day," he said, then paused and gathered his courage. "The second one will out me to the world, Barb. And there's no going back from that."

"That song you just played is Sebastian Hunter's goodbye to his dead mother. Of course it's fucking sad! As for outing you, well…" Barb stood up. "It's about damn time. You've never been a coward, Ethan. Your shit will probably sell like crazy, afterwards. Women like unattainable men, you know." She nodded decisively. "I'll book studio time in the next city for the song you just played me. We'll get it on the air in a few weeks. It doesn't need to be fancy. In fact, it *shouldn't* be fancy. It just needs to be *done.* You should decide if you want to do the second song, too. If so, we can release it a few weeks after the first one. That's good marketing."

"But what about Sebastian?" Ethan asked. His heart knocked against his ribs. The thought of seeing him again made him sweat.

"We'll credit him, of course. And he'll get paid, as he should've been for all the music he helped his mother write. And maybe this will get him out of whatever shit job he's in and back where he belongs, in the studio," Barb said, as if it were a done deal. "As for you and him—be a man, Ethan, and do the right fucking thing," she said, heading for the door. "You know what you have to do."

Chapter Five

Sebastian stood outside the theatre wondering just what in the hell he thought he was doing. His hands were sweaty, and he gripped the tickets as if they would disappear if he so much as breathed wrong.

"Sebastian, get a grip on yourself," Darlene said, digging fingers into his bicep. "Are you going in, or not? Because if you're not going in, I'm going without you. There is no way I'm missing a Duke Clementine performance. He's one of my two favorite singers." She grinned. "I have no idea how one family managed to produce two brilliant artists in one generation, but I'm not going to complain about it. I saw his cousin, Vin, perform just a couple months ago."

Sebastian looked up at the old building and shook his head at his friend. "I don't even know what we're doing here. This kind of thing is for industry people and die-hard fans."

"Dude, I *am* a die-hard fan," Darlene said. "When Duke's cousin got married, I cried. Remember? Marvin Clementine's wife is one lucky chick."

He gave her a look, not nearly as cheerful as she was, and she sighed.

"Tell me something I don't know, Sebastian. The scalper on the corner was selling one ticket for a thousand bucks." Darlene tried to tug him towards the doors. "Come on. I'm never in my life going to get to see Duke Clementine this up close and personal again. You're are *not* going to chicken out and deprive me of this."

Sebastian let Darlene tow him to the line. "This is crazy."

"Someday you're going to have to tell me how you got the tickets, because 'I won them from a radio station' is a lie. I know all of your tells," she said, smiling at the security guard. The guy winked at her as he searched her purse.

Of course she doesn't believe me, Sebastian thought, flushing. He flashed back to an image of Ethan's after-sex face from all those months ago. For some reason, he couldn't get that day out of his head. He cleared his throat, willing his half hard cock to calm the hell down.

"Are you going to spit it out, or just stand there looking constipated?" Darlene asked. "Tell me how you got the tickets."

Sebastian rolled his eyes. "Okay, fine. Duke Clementine was the client on that flight to Mumbai." Using Ethan's stage name felt weird and impersonal. He pressed his tongue against the back of his teeth.

"Wait, what? Your first job with the company? And you got him to send you tickets to his show? I thought maybe you pulled some strings because I know your mom had been a musician," Darlene said, eyebrows raised. "Also, shit. I can't believe I had to miss that flight. It figures."

I'm glad she missed it, though it sucks that her sister was sick, Sebastian thought, very privately. He was glad not because he didn't like his friend, but because otherwise, there was no way he and Ethan would've hooked up. "He's a really nice guy."

"Nice?" Darlene snorted as they slowly moved forward in line. "Duke Clementine isn't anything as simple as nice, dude. He's pure sex, Sebastian. Sex on two legs. I'll probably faint if he looks at me."

That might be a problem then, Sebastian thought, finally amused. Ethan had sent them front row tickets. He ignored the heat prickling at the base of his spine at the thought of seeing Ethan again, live and in person instead of stalking him on the internet like he'd been doing. He'd told absolutely no one about what'd happened, either the music they'd written together or the sex. The man deserved his privacy. And Sebastian needed the memory to remain pure. He'd never betray Ethan's trust.

"So, you used to tour with your mom, right?" Darlene asked as they made their way to their seats. "You've probably been here before."

Sebastian nodded. "She didn't tour that much, but yeah. I've been in this theatre before. It has great acoustics." He led her down the aisle to the front row. Stage hands were busy taping down wires as they did some last-minute prep on the stage. He smiled, remembering what it had been like to hang out with his mother when she traveled. He'd loved it. She hadn't gone on the road all the time because she'd never been super famous, but they'd managed to get around the world a couple times. *I miss her.*

"Okay, whoa. We're in the front row? Seriously?" Darlene's voice rose alarmingly.

Sebastian laughed. "Yeah. Surprise."

"What. The. Fuck. Sebastian," she said, gripping his arm as they sat down. She glanced around. "This is amazing. What did you do to get these seats, give him a blowjob?" She smirked, obviously teasing him.

If only she knew. Sebastian stared at her for a moment, and then looked away, heat washing over his face. *Shit. She's going to figure it out if I don't keep it together better than this.*

"Oh my *God,* I was joking!" Darlene hissed, eyes wide. "I thought he was straight!"

"Shh!" Sebastian looked around. Luckily no one was paying any attention to them. "I don't know what you're talking about. I didn't say anything!"

"You don't have to! Your face said it for me. I

know you, Sebastian," Darlene countered, eyes wild. "Is this why you've been moping around the past few months? Jesus, please tell me you didn't fall in love with the guy?"

Sebastian ignored her. He sat down and smoothed a nervous hand over the armrest. This particular theatre was small and intimate, and more suited to small performances than the kind of huge venues that Duke Clementine usually played. *When he comes on stage, we're going to be staring right at each other.* He didn't know if his heart could take it.

"Sebastian, seriously." Darlene tugged on his sleeve. "You can't drop that kind of bomb into the conversation and expect me to just ignore it!"

Sebastian grimaced, taking her hand. "Darlene, please, let it go," he said, hoping she listened to him. From the look on her face, it wasn't going to happen. "It was months ago, and he was a *client,* so you know I can't talk about anything that happened on the plane." He shook his head. "And more than that, he is a very good man. I'm not going to gossip about him." *And besides, how could I possibly have fallen in love in one day? That only happens in novels, and usually tragic ones, at that,* he thought, running a hand over his face. He was nervous. Obviously, Ethan remembered him, or he wouldn't have sent him these tickets. So, what did that mean?

"Sebastian—"

"No." Sebastian cut her off before she could speculate anymore. "I can't talk about it, Darlene. You know that."

She frowned at him, but Sebastian shook his head. "Just enjoy the show, okay?"

Darlene glared at him for another moment, but then she sighed and patted his arm. "Fine. But you know

I'll find out eventually."

Sebastian rolled his eyes. "Yeah, yeah. Maybe when we're old and grey."

She poked him in the arm. "You can't keep a secret from me, Sebastian. I'm your best friend, remember."

I kept a secret from you for three months, he wanted to say, but then the band wandered onto the stage. The lights dimmed, and the audience quieted as they waited for Duke to appear.

"Oh, man. I'm so freaking excited!" Darlene whispered. She bumped her shoulder into Sebastian's bicep. "I've loved his music for forever, plus he's hot."

"Me too," Sebastian replied, blushing again. His nerves hadn't settled, but it didn't matter. He was here. He was going to see Ethan up close and amplified, and he could barely sit still. He'd kept tabs on him, and knew that this particular stop hadn't been in the original tour lineup. He had no idea why Ethan had added it on, but he couldn't deny that he was pretty damned excited. Getting to see Ethan sing live, this close up, with a small acoustic band was definitely a once in a lifetime event. He knew a lot of industry people were here—he'd recognized a few as they'd found their seats, though they hadn't recognized him. He'd been young when he'd worked with his mother, and then she'd died, and he'd grown up way too fucking fast. He sighed. The pang of grief was smaller now, but still there. He rubbed his chest, and then his heart gave a hard thump. Ethan was walking across the darkened stage to the microphone set on top of a large Persian rug. Some of the people in the audience stood up and cheered, but Sebastian couldn't seem to get his legs to work.

God, Ethan is right here in front of me, he thought wildly. When the lights came on, their gazes met. Sebastian stopped breathing when Ethan smiled, blue eyes as electric as he remembered.

Of course he's still fucking gorgeous, Sebastian thought, staring at Ethan's too-tight leather pants and his red shirt, half unbuttoned. His heart pounded. He remembered what it had been like to run his hands through Ethan's hair, and he had to curl his fingers into fists or God only knew what he'd do.

"Holy shit, Sebastian, he's staring at you!" Darlene said, shaking him. "You're still sitting? Get up. Come on." She tried to pull him up, but he couldn't move.

Ethan tapped the microphone, and the band's bass player plucked the E string. The sound reverberated through the theatre. Darlene tightened her fingers around Sebastian's shoulder hard enough to hurt. Sebastian extricated himself from her grip, and when he looked up again, Ethan was still looking at him. His blue eyes seemed lit from within, and Sebastian had the feeling that Ethan was nervous, though he hid it well. The man had been performing for years, after all.

"Good evening," Ethan said into the microphone. His smooth voice slid over Sebastian's skin like warm honey, and he shivered. The crowd went wild. Everyone still sitting leaped to their feet. Ethan, however, kept on staring right at him. He didn't even pretend to look anywhere else, just kept his steady blue gaze fixed on Sebastian. "Thank you for coming to this impromptu gig."

Wait. Is he talking to me? Sebastian slowly rose. All the feelings he'd tried so hard to bury in the last few months surged forward. He wanted to climb up on stage and kiss the hell out of Ethan. He wanted to run his hands over Ethan's smooth skin and lick every tattoo. He wanted to bury himself in the man until neither of them knew where one began and the other ended. He stared back, almost daring Ethan to do something. *Stop it, idiot. As far as everyone knows, he's straight, and he's not going to out himself on stage in the middle of a sold-out tour. It would be career suicide.*

"I wrote a couple new songs a few months ago. I'm going to sing the first one for you now," Ethan said, and then he tilted his head. "Actually, I wrote both of them with someone, which is unusual for me, as you know, but it was an unusual circumstance, with an unusual man."

Sebastian froze. What the hell was Ethan up to? He licked his lips, and Ethan smirked at him. Sebastian raised his eyebrows—*what are you doing?*—and Ethan smiled, slow and sexy. Darlene sighed next to him, and Sebastian couldn't blame her. Ethan was one hell of a sexy man.

"The man I wrote this song with is sitting in the audience tonight. It's a tribute to his mother, Sue Hunter, one of the greatest songwriters of her generation," Ethan said, blue eyes steady on Sebastian. "I hope you like it," he said, ostensibly to the audience, but Sebastian knew for sure this time that Ethan was speaking directly to him. The musician gestured to the band, and they launched into the opening chords that Sebastian and Ethan had worked on all those months ago.

And then, fucking Duke Clementine began to sing.

"Oh, you bastard," Sebastian murmured, mesmerized. He ignored Darlene's excited exclamation. He couldn't look away from the stage. Ethan's voice carried the song from the slowest, sweetest beginning to an impossible soaring note that only he could have managed. By the time the song was over, Sebastian was crying, because every word, every note reminded him of his mother. Afterwards, Ethan smiled at Sebastian, and then launched into an acoustic version of his latest hit, finally looking away and playing to the rest of the people in the theatre.

As the rest of the audience began to sit back down to enjoy the acoustic set, Sebastian sank down, gripping the armrests as if they would keep him from flying off and away. He felt like he was on a ship in the midst of a turbulent sea.

"Oh, you have *so much* to tell me, Sebastian," Darlene said, leaning close to his ear.

He chanced a glance at her, and she grinned at him, because she *knew* something had gone down with him and Ethan. She wasn't stupid. He shrugged, but she shook her head and turned her attention back to the stage.

I'm so fucked, he thought. On stage, Ethan caught his eye again and lifted his shoulder slightly. It was sexy as hell, and all Sebastian could do was grit his teeth and ignore the hard-on pressing into the zipper of his jeans.

****

Two hours and one short intermission later, Ethan settled down on a stool in the center of the stage. Sebastian was exhausted just from watching, so he knew Ethan had to be completely wiped, not that anyone could tell. He looked just as charismatic now as he had when he'd first stepped on stage. Over the past few hours, Ethan had stroked the audience from hushed awe to foot stomping excitement and back down again. At some point, he'd changed his shirt from red to silver, and the new hue brought out the blue in his eyes. Sebastian couldn't tear his gaze away.

When Ethan quietly picked up the acoustic guitar Sebastian remembered from the plane, a frisson of anxiety shot through him. When he saw the rest of the band file off the stage, he sat up, muscles so tight he couldn't stand up right now even if he wanted to. He'd just fall back down again. "What the hell is he doing?" he murmured, but Darlene hushed him.

"Shh. I had no idea this show was going to be so long. This is amazing," she said, excitement clear in her voice.

Sebastian frowned. She seemed to think that the next song was going to be just an ordinary part of the set, but Sebastian knew better. It was the end of the show. Musicians *never* sent the rest of the band away in order to do an acoustic song alone, at the very end of the night. This was when bands ramped up the volume and the energy for the finale. They didn't quiet it down. *Not unless there's something more going on here,* he thought, thinking of all the countless concerts he'd attended with his mother.

Ethan raised his hand and the audience quieted. "This song is special and true." He cleared his throat, and strummed a chord, then readjusted the capo he'd placed on the frets. For a moment he looked like he was going to launch into a complex explanation, and Sebastian held his breath, but then Ethan simply said, "This song is for Sebastian."

"Oh my God," Darlene whispered, but Sebastian barely noticed. He was too busy holding his breath as Ethan looked directly at him and started to sing. The lyrics washed over him as Ethan's voice, warm and husky for just this song, slid into his heart and yanked him awake. Sebastian gripped the armrests, heart in his throat as Ethan sang about meeting a boy and falling in love. And then, just when he couldn't take it anymore, Ethan sang about falling in love with *Sebastian,* and the crowd was so silent you could've heard a pin drop. Sebastian found himself standing, pushing against the stage as if he could climb up right there, right now. His heart had lodged up against his ribs, hopeful and frightened at the same time, but he held Ethan's gaze. How could he not?

When the last note faded, in the middle of the mad applause from the crowd, Ethan set the guitar down and came to the edge of the stage. He knelt down, ignoring the cell phones and camera flashes recording him. "Sebastian." He reached out.

Slowly, Sebastian put his hands in Ethan's. The man grabbed him, and hauled him up where everyone could see, and pulled him into an embrace. "What the hell, Ethan?" Sebastian said, wincing when Ethan's microphone picked up his words. He looked around. How did they get to the center of the stage?

"You know what the hell, Sebastian," Ethan said, laughing, and then he drew him into a kiss.

Sebastian thought maybe he'd died and gone to heaven. Ethan tasted like lightning and thunder, and completely, utterly familiar. He tasted like home. Sebastian kissed him back with all the pent-up longing and desperation he'd pretended hadn't existed for the past few months. From the way Ethan responded, he felt the same way. When they finally came up for air, the crowd was cheering. Sebastian flushed as he leaned his forehead on Ethan's. "Dude. You just outed yourself." The microphone was still on, but Sebastian figured it didn't matter at this point. There was no way anyone was going to mistake that blistering kiss for something platonic.

Ethan nodded. "So I did. You know I don't do things halfway." He grinned. "So, I wanted to know, do you want this?" He gestured to the stage and the audience, and then at himself. "Because I've been going through the motions without you, and it isn't enough. I want the real thing, Sebastian." Ethan kissed him, quick and soft. "I want to write more music with you and I want to wake up in the morning next to you and I want your face to be the last thing I see after the show's done, and it's time to go back to sleep."

Sebastian's heart thumped so hard he couldn't focus. "Ethan," he breathed. "Way to give me a heart attack."

"The music isn't the same without you," Ethan whispered. "Tell me you want it, too."

Sebastian's eyes prickled. "Yeah." He stopped and cleared his throat. "Of course I want it." He inhaled, nervous and relieved and so fucking turned on he could barely speak. "I want you."

Ethan exhaled noisily. "Thank fuck." He kissed him again.

Sebastian ignored the audience freaking out and sank his hands into Ethan's hair. "I'll have to quit my job."

"Dude, you're going to be writing music with me. And you play piano, right? As well as guitar?" Ethan asked, and then he grinned. "And fucking viola, of all things."

"How did you know that?" Sebastian leaned back.

Ethan smiled wickedly, then looked over Sebastian's shoulder. "Put up the clip, Joe."

Sebastian frowned, and then a huge projected image of him playing piano for his mother lit up the back of the stage. He looked about thirteen. "Oh no. Is this the one where I'm singing—"

Ethan cut him off. "Yup."

Sebastian thunked his head down on Ethan's shoulder. "You're going to pay for this."

Ethan laughed. The Sebastian in the clip started singing. He sounded young, but also not half bad. He remembered that day. He'd sung the happy birthday song to his mom. "You are a dead man," he told Ethan.

"I'll make it up to you," Ethan said, voice low and sexy.

Sebastian shivered. "Are you sure about this? We don't really know each other."

Ethan nodded. "I'm sure. I knew the moment we started writing together that you were it for me."

"Love at first sight?" Sebastian asked.

Ethan tilted his head as teen Sebastian sang on in the background. Someone had had the decency to cut Ethan's mike, so at least their conversation wasn't being broadcast to the entire audience. "Sebastian, love isn't a single moment. It's a journey." He cupped Sebastian's face. "And we started that trip back on the plane."

Sebastian chewed on his lip. "True story."

Ethan's expression slipped a bit, then. "But I just want you to know what you're getting into. What you're giving up." He gestured to the stage, and the audience. "You understand, right?"

Sebastian nodded. He knew Ethan's lifestyle wasn't easy, and it wasn't private. If they did this, every moment they shared in public was going to be plastered in high definition all over the world. He'd be willing to bet that the embrace they'd just shared was already out there.

Ethan kissed him again. "I'm not giving anything up except loneliness. The question is, are you sure that you know what you'd be getting into? You have to tell me, in words." He waited a beat. "Please say something, Sebastian."

Sebastian let himself think about it for a hot second: spend the next several years catering to spoiled, rich clients as a flight attendant, or spend the rest of his life figuring out what love truly was with Ethan. *Easy question to answer,* he realized. "Yeah," he said, voice cracking. "I know."

Ethan exhaled, long and low. "Thank God."

Sebastian smiled. "Bit nervous, eh?"

"You have no idea," Ethan said, with feeling.

Sebastian gripped his biceps, enjoying the feeling of Ethan vibrating beneath his fingers. "Oh, I think I might have a clue, Ethan." He grinned and stepped back. "This isn't my first concert, you know." He touched Ethan's guitar. It felt like an old, long forgotten friend.

Ethan rolled his eyes. "Enough flirting. Play us a song, Sebastian." He tapped the microphone. "Play something sweet." His voice echoed through the theatre. The sound system was back on.

Sebastian put the guitar's strap over his head and settled it on his shoulder. He strummed a few chords experimentally, and then he smiled as he looked out over the audience. Standing up here with Ethan felt good. He wasn't even the least bit nervous anymore. "Sweet?" He shook his head at Ethan. "No. But I'll play you something sexy," he said, and launched into the opening riff of one of his favorite Duke Clementine songs: a sleeper from the man's first album. It hadn't been a popular hit, but among musicians it ranked high on the list of most excellent songs. When his lover smirked, clearly unsurprised, Sebastian added a few extra notes, playing with the melody in a way that only someone completely comfortable on stage could. It had been a long time for him, but Sebastian remembered this feeling well. He'd missed it. He grinned and Ethan started singing, and nothing had ever felt so right.

Epilogue

"So, that went well," Ethan said, pulling Sebastian into his dressing room. He ignored the food and the sofa, and shoved Sebastian up against the door. He'd been hard for hours, and his cock ached. Judging from Sebastian's expression, the younger man wasn't much better off right now.

"You're insane, you know. You could've just called me. Like, on the phone," Sebastian said, hands going for Ethan's shirt. "You didn't have to do the whole grand coming out thing onstage, in front of the whole world."

"But what if I wanted to do the grand gesture?" Ethan undid Sebastian's pants and slipped a hand inside to press over his erection. "You're worth the grand gesture, Sebastian."

Sebastian moaned and ripped Ethan's shirt open. Buttons scattered everywhere.

"Holy shit, Sebastian," Ethan said, swallowing hard as the younger man pressed into him.

Sebastian shook his head. "I never thought I'd see you again, so I'm feeling a bit desperate here." He pushed his hips forward. "There's no going back now, Ethan."

Ethan nearly lost his handful of Sebastian's cock as his lover writhed against him. "God. Okay, okay," he muttered tugging at Sebastian's shirt and pants. A minute later, he hadn't gotten anywhere. Both of them were still mostly clothed. Sebastian kept rolling his hips forward, dislodging his grip. "I'm going to come in my pants," he said, voice ragged.

"Same." Sebastian dropped his head to Ethan's shoulder, but he stopped thrusting. "I'm so fucking close it isn't even funny."

"Come on." With a supreme effort, Ethan stepped back. He locked the door, then stripped off his clothes. When Sebastian didn't move, and instead stood there staring at him, he grinned. "Get with the program, Sebastian." He checked the clock on the wall. "We don't have a lot of time."

Sebastian groaned, but obediently took off his clothes. When he was naked, he stalked forward and dragged Ethan into a kiss.

Ethan was totally okay with that, but he also wanted more. "Here. Over here," he said, dragging his lover to the sofa. It was red leather, and worn thin on the arms, but none of that mattered. He bent over and looked over his shoulder at Sebastian. "Fuck me."

Sebastian's nostrils flared. "Are you crazy?"

Ethan snorted. "I will be if you don't put your cock exactly where I want it."

Sebastian stalked over, erection bouncing. He looked delicious. Ethan's own cock grew harder, and he reached down to stroke himself.

"Lube? Condoms?" Sebastian asked.

"Condoms are there," Ethan said, jerking his head at the side table. The bowl of colorful condoms was often standard fare in these back rooms, but this would be the first time he'd indulged in years.

"You look like everything I've ever wanted," Sebastian said, stepping closer. He put a hand on Ethan's hip and leaned down to kiss him in the middle of his spine.

Ethan shivered as Sebastian's breath warmed his skin. "You can have me," he growled, wishing the man would get on with it. They'd have time for slow and sweet later. Right now, he wanted it fast and dirty. "Come *on,* Sebastian. Fuck me."

Sebastian took himself in hand, and bumped up against Ethan's ass. "You're sure?"

Ethan reared up, about to force the issue, but then Sebastian grabbed his hips and pressed against his hole. "Oh motherfucker, Ethan. You're slick. How in the hell?" He groaned, long and low as his cock slid inside. "Jesus."

"I prepped before I got on stage," Ethan gasped, shuddering at the burn.

Sebastian gripped Ethan's hips hard enough to bruise. "Wait. You mean you were lubed and loose the entire time you were on stage?"

Ethan nodded. "Yup."

Sebastian's hips snapped forward all at once, and Ethan moaned. The man knew exactly what he was doing. Sparks flew behind his eyelids as Sebastian's cock hit his prostate. "You are going to be the death of me," Sebastian said, punctuating his words with tiny thrusts.

Ethan didn't have the capacity to reply. He shivered, clenching his inner muscles.

Sebastian panted, and then began fucking him in earnest. "So close, Ethan. I'm not gonna last."

Ethan shook his head. "Me neither." He hung onto the sofa with both hands as Sebastian's movements grew increasingly erratic. "Come on, babe. Give it to me."

"That's what I'm doing," Sebastian said through clenched teeth. He moved faster, slick skin on slick skin, and suddenly, without warning, Ethan's orgasm rushed through him. He threw his head back as electricity sparked through him, and Sebastian pushed in one last time, hips jerking. "Fuck, fuck," he muttered, but Ethan couldn't reply. His cock jerked, painting the old leather beneath him with jizz. He'd never climaxed without anyone touching his cock, and he sucked in air as his muscles trembled. Another wave of pleasure shot through him, and then it was like someone cut his strings. His knees collapsed, and they landed on the sofa together, limbs askew even as they hung onto each other.

"Holy shit," Sebastian said when they'd finally caught their breath. His brown eyes gleamed as he leaned his forehead against Ethan's shoulder.

"No shit," Ethan replied, firmly echoing the sentiment. He knew exactly what Sebastian meant. He stroked a hand down his lover's arm.

Across the room, someone pounded on the door. "Ethan! Unlock this door! I've got the media breathing down my damned throat!" Barb's voice was probably the only one that could penetrate the post-orgasmic haze in Ethan's head.

He snorted. "Duty calls," he said, beginning the process of extricating himself from Sebastian.

"Who is that?" Sebastian looked worried when Barb banged on the door again.

"I have a key, you know!" she yelled.

"My manager slash assistant. Don't worry. She's not angry," Ethan said to Sebastian, giving him a quick kiss. "Trust me. I was ready for this." He took a deep breath. "Give me a few minutes, Barb!" he yelled to his manager. He'd finally managed to stand up. Drying semen decorated his abdomen and hip. *This is going to be a fun cleanup,* he thought, amused.

"I'm a hot mess." Sebastian made a face as he tied off the used condom. He glanced at Ethan. "And so are you. Everyone is going to know exactly what we were doing." He looked down at himself in despair, one hand holding the condom, and the other trying unsuccessfully to wipe a stray bit of jizz from his leg.

"They already know, Sebastian," Ethan said, cracking open a bottle of water. He poured it onto a wad of napkins and handed them over, then did the same for himself. Five minutes later they'd managed to dress and hide most of the evidence. Ethan knew there was no way to disguise the hickey on his neck, especially on such short notice, and he didn't much care. "And it was totally worth it. You ready?" he asked Sebastian. The younger man had just smoothed down his short hair. "You look great. Stop fussing." He ran a hand through his own messy locks.

Sebastian smiled wryly at him. "I guess this is it, huh?"

Ethan nodded. "It is. You ready?"

"Yeah." Sebastian looked at the door, and then he turned to Ethan. He looked hot and sexy and like everything a rock star should, which was awesome, because that's what he was about to become, if Ethan had any say in the matter. Sebastian had talent, and Ethan intended on dragging it out into the light.

"All right then," Ethan murmured, heart full of words he didn't have the time to offer right now.

Sebastian smiled as if he already knew them all. "Let's do this."

****

"To no one's surprise, Duke Clementine and Sebastian Hunter's first collaborative album is set to debut on next week's Hot 100 album chart at number one. Sources say it's just the beginning for this electric duo, and music fans are champing at the bit since samples of the first single leaked online just a few short days ago. So far, the two men haven't released a statement about the leak, but that's hardly surprising as they're still on honeymoon in Aruba. Photos show the duo can't stop singing, even while on vacation. Customers of a karaoke bar on the beach certainly had a shock when the two got up to perform the hit song Duke

Clementine debuted at his acoustic concert six months ago." — *Hot Pop Press*

The End

www.erinmleaf.com

EVERNIGHT PUBLISHING ®

www.evernightpublishing.com